W9-AUL-162

**"There are two things I know for sure,"
he began. "One—and this is probably
the most important—you are going to
make an amazing mother."**

She looked up at him with those big eyes and his
heart stuttered.

"Two. We'll figure out how to take care of those
babies together. We'll make mistakes but they won't
be the same ones as our folks. I can guarantee that
much."

"How are we going to do that, Rory?" There was a
straight-up challenge in her eyes.

He didn't say by keeping a safe distance or by not
kissing her again.

Because that was exactly what he did—kissed her.

"You're not making this easy." He said the words
low as his mouth moved against hers when he
spoke.

But great sex wasn't going to help the situation.

And the sound of a twig crunching nearby sent his
pulse racing.

BULLETPROOF CHRISTMAS

USA TODAY Bestselling Author

BARB HAN

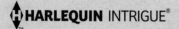
HARLEQUIN INTRIGUE®

If you purchased this book without a cover you should be aware that this book is stolen property. It was reported as "unsold and destroyed" to the publisher, and neither the author nor the publisher has received any payment for this "stripped book."

All my love to Brandon, Jacob and Tori. And to all the grand adventures that lay ahead.

To Babe, my bulletproof hero, for being my great love, my place to call home. This life is everything.

ISBN-13: 978-1-335-63957-8

Bulletproof Christmas

Copyright © 2018 by Barb Han

PLEASE RECYCLE · THIS PRODUCT IS RECYCLABLE

Recycling programs for this product may not exist in your area.

All rights reserved. Except for use in any review, the reproduction or utilization of this work in whole or in part in any form by any electronic, mechanical or other means, now known or hereafter invented, including xerography, photocopying and recording, or in any information storage or retrieval system, is forbidden without the written permission of the publisher, Harlequin Enterprises Limited, 22 Adelaide St. West, 40th Floor, Toronto, Ontario M5H 4E3, Canada.

This is a work of fiction. Names, characters, places and incidents are either the product of the author's imagination or are used fictitiously, and any resemblance to actual persons, living or dead, business establishments, events or locales is entirely coincidental.

This edition published by arrangement with Harlequin Books S.A.

For questions and comments about the quality of this book, please contact us at CustomerService@Harlequin.com.

® and TM are trademarks of Harlequin Enterprises Limited or its corporate affiliates. Trademarks indicated with ® are registered in the United States Patent and Trademark Office, the Canadian Intellectual Property Office and in other countries.

Printed in U.S.A.

HARLEQUIN®
™ www.Harlequin.com

USA TODAY bestselling author **Barb Han** lives in north Texas with her very own hero-worthy husband, three beautiful children, a spunky golden retriever/ standard poodle mix and too many books in her to-read pile. In her downtime, she plays video games and spends much of her time on or around a basketball court. She loves interacting with readers and is grateful for their support. You can reach her at barbhan.com.

Visit the Author Profile page at Harlequin.com.

CAST OF CHARACTERS

Cadence Butler—This youngest Butler heir has been hiding her pregnancy for six months. What other secrets is she keeping?

Rory Scott—He's a tracker by trade and a man who lives for the range.

Rupert Grinnell—This ranch hand might've been hired on last but does he know the most?

Martin Jenkins—How much does this cousin of Rupert's know about Maverick Mike's death?

Randol Fleming—And what connection does this cousin of Rupert's have to Maverick Mike's death?

Dex Henley—How does this friend of Rupert's fit into the picture?

Sheriff Clarence Sawmill—This sheriff might be in over his head with a high-profile murder to solve and a town in chaos.

Maverick Mike Butler—Even in death, this self-made Texas rancher has a few cards left to play.

Chapter One

Patience. Silence. Purpose. The mantra had kept Rory Scott alive while tracking some of the most ruthless poachers in the country. Belly crawling toward a makeshift campsite on the Hereford Ranch in Cattle Barge, Texas, he adjusted his night-vision goggles to gain a better view and evaluate the situation.

A two-person tent was set up twenty-five feet ahead and slightly to his left. It looked expensive, like it was from one of those stores in the city that overcharged for basic camping supplies, promising to guard people from the elements or turn desk jockeys into outdoorsmen with the right backpack.

A campfire was spitting blue-and-yellow embers into the frigid night air not ten feet away from a brown-and-beige pop-up tent. The light coming from the blaze would be a beacon to anyone who might be traveling in the area. Of course, this was private property so there shouldn't have been anyone around. The Hereford Ranch was one of the rare few in Texas that was successful enough selling cattle that the owners weren't forced to lease parts of the land for hunting. The land and mineral rights were owned by one of the wealthiest families in the state, the Butlers. Rory had personal knowledge that no one had been given permission to be there. This campsite was a trespassing violation at the very least, possibly more.

A law meant to crack down on illegal hunting made it a felony offense to poach on someone's land. And that sifted out the less-experienced thrill-seekers. The pros upped the ante, which also made them more dangerous than ever. Rory didn't mind putting his life on the line for a good cause since he didn't doubt his skills and could net a bigger paycheck because of the increased risk. Besides, he had no one at home waiting for him to return and that was the way he liked living life.

This campsite looked set up for a romantic rendezvous but Rory had too much experience to take anything at face value. He wouldn't put anything past a skilled poacher. This whole scenario could be cover for a scout, someone who fed information to poachers.

Surveying the perimeter, Rory located a small bag of trash tied to a tree roughly ten yards away from the campsite. Every experienced outdoorsman knew to hang his trash far away from his campsite or risk attracting dangerous wildlife searching for an easy meal. By contrast, most didn't shop at those overpriced stores.

Rory took a breath of fresh Texas air in his lungs. He'd been working on a ranch in Wyoming for the past five months while trying to keep his thoughts away from the woman he'd walked away from. Time was supposed to give perspective. He sighed sharply. Clearly, it would take more than five months to rid his mind of Cadence Butler.

When her brother Dade had called to say he needed the best tracker, Rory wasted no time getting on the road.

Of course, the Butlers didn't know he was coming. He'd refused the job with his friends because it was best that no one—and that included the Butler family—knew he'd be onsite. Not just because of his past relationship with Cadence. *Relationship?* That was probably a strong word. More like *history.* It was their history that had caused him to momentarily lose his grip on reality by spending one too many nights with the off-limits heiress. Keeping the family, and everyone else, in the dark would give him the element of surprise. If one of the Butlers knew he was coming, word could get out.

Dade wouldn't have called if he'd known about the fling. Rory and Cadence had kept their relationship on the quiet side, or so he had thought until her father confronted him. The charismatic Maverick Mike Butler had been right about one thing: Rory had no business seeing the man's daughter. She was out of his league and Cadence would never survive his lifestyle of living on the range, being constantly on the go.

The thought of settling into one spot made Rory's collar shrink. He had a cabin built for one in Texas near Cattle Barge that he called home. One was his lucky number.

No matter what else, it was best that the Butlers had no idea he'd be around. One slip would cause word to get out, since a small family-oriented place like Cattle Barge wasn't known for being able to keep a secret. Hell, the town's business had been plastered across every newspaper for months ever since Maverick Mike Butler's murder last summer, which Rory was truly sorry for when he'd found out about it. Mr. Butler had given Rory a job when he was lost and alone at fifteen years old. Rory had kept his life on the straight and narrow because of the opportunity he'd been given and he would go to his own grave grateful for the hand up when he'd been down on his luck and searching for a steady place to land. Rory had never minded hard work, and Mr. Butler's only caveat for keeping his job had been that Rory finish high school.

He had, and his boss had attended his graduation. He'd patted Rory on the back and told him he was proud of him.

Granted, the man didn't like Rory having anything to do with Cadence. But Rory couldn't blame a father for wanting to protect his daughter. Maverick Mike seemed to know on instinct the same fact Rory had surmised early on—that he'd only cause Cadence heartache.

Even though her father had had harsh words for him, Rory respected the man who'd grown up a sharecropper's son but made good on his life.

His heart went out to the family for their loss and his thoughts often wound to Cadence in the months since, wondering how she was handling the news.

Being in Cattle Barge and thinking about the past caused memories of his parents' volatile marriage to resurface. Heavy weights bore down on his shoulders and it was doing nothing to improve his sour mood.

To make matters worse, Christmas was around the corner. He'd lost touch with his sister, Renee, who was the only other sane person in the family. She'd split at seventeen years old, and then he took off shortly after. The holidays made him think about her, wonder where she was now and if she was happy.

Rory shook off the emotions wrapping a heavy blanket around him. No good ever came of thinking about his family or the empty holiday he faced being alone. He reminded himself that it was his choice to be by himself. He had no use for distractions.

He performed a mental headshake in hopes of clearing his mind. Surveying the campsite again, he skimmed the area for signs of people. It was cold tonight and he doubted the warmth from the fire would be enough. A piece of material meant to secure the tent flapped with the wind. Inside, it was empty.

Rory rolled a few times on the cold earth.

His movement stealth-like and with purpose. This vantage point allowed him a better view inside the small tent. There were two sleeping bags that had been placed next to each other inside.

Being back on Butler land made him think about the time he and Cadence had stayed up all night talking in her father's barn. It was the first time he realized his feelings were careening out of control. Because staying up all night with a woman *to talk* had never held a lot of appeal before her. Cadence was the perfect mix of intelligence, sass and sense of humor. She was always on the go and sometimes acted before she thought something through, but her heart was always in the right place. His chest clutched while he thought about her. He needed to stop himself right there. That was the past. *She* was the past. The best way to end up thrown from his horse was to keep looking backward.

Besides, nothing could be changed and he'd only end up with a crick in his neck.

A log crackled, sending another round of burning embers into the air. Rory hoped like hell the couple who'd lit it didn't have plans to go to sleep with the blaze still going, *if* there was a couple. There was no accounting for lack of skill and knowledge. If this was a situation with inexperienced campers they might not even realize they'd set up on private property. A place as massive as Hereford was impossible to cordon off completely from the outside world, even though security would be tighter following Mr. Butler's murder.

Rory changed position again, moving stealthily along the tree line near the lake. He crouched behind the trunk of a mesquite tree, watching, waiting. A blast of frigid air penetrated straight through his winter jacket. It was twelve in the morning, which could be considered early or late, depending on point of view. Tomorrow was supposed to be even colder. The mornings were already crisp and the forecast said a cold front was moving in for Christmas Eve in five days.

He shouldn't complain. This was nothing compared to December weather in Wyoming. Forty degrees was practically a heat wave.

The twenty-hours-straight drive had tied Rory's muscles into knots. They were screaming to be stretched. Exhaustion and cold slowed his reflexes. He'd have to take that into account if he confronted the campers.

Protecting the Butler property took top priority for reasons he didn't want to examine.

He'd known the family since he was a kid. His father had worked in the barn for part of Rory's childhood before blowing up at his boss and getting fired. Rory had plenty of fond memories of spending time with the twins, Dalton and Dade. The Butler boys had treated him like one of them from the very beginning. That was most likely the reason he felt compelled to take this job and why he felt so damn guilty for having the fling with Cadence.

Rory could rest later when he turned over the bad guys and collected his paycheck.

At this time of night, the campers should have been in their tent. The wind had picked up and Rory was certain the temperature had dropped ten degrees in the last hour.

Moving silently along the perimeter of their camp, he repositioned away from the water, noting that this location was a little too close to the Butler home for comfort.

A noise on the opposite side, the place where he'd first set up, caught his attention. Rory flattened his body against the cold hard earth. Wind whipped the fire around as he flexed and released his fingers to keep blood flowing.

A man came into view of the firelight. He had to be roughly five feet ten inches, if Rory had to guess, a good four inches shorter than him. The guy had on jogging pants, tennis shoes and a dark hoodie. A smallish dog— on closer inspection, it looked like a beagle mix—trotted behind City Guy's heels. That was bad news for Rory because the dog would pick up his scent and give away his location. Even with the fierce winds, it was only a matter of time before the beagle found him.

To avoid that fiasco, he would make himself known. He hopped to his feet and moved about fifteen feet closer before making a loud grunting noise to call attention to his presence. He needed a good reason to be out there alone this time of night...

"Dammit," he said loudly as he stalked out of the shadows, making as much noise as one man could without a herd of elephants behind him. "I seem to have lost my hunting knife. It was a present from my girlfriend and things haven't been so great between us lately. I really don't want to have to go home and explain that. There's no chance you've seen it, is there?"

From this distance, Rory could see the man's face had a day's worth of stubble and he was wearing one of those expensive compass watches. No way was this an outdoorsman.

City Guy seemed thrown by Rory's presence, making him believe the man was either up to no good or scared out of his wits. Poachers were generally harder to detect and it usually took days, sometimes weeks, to track them. They rarely ever set up camp unless they were armed to the nines or stupid, and the latter were easily caught.

The man quickly recovered a casual disposition, bending down to grab his dog by the collar. He took a knee next to the beagle. "Sorry, what did you say you're looking for?"

"A knife about so-big." Rory made a show of holding his hands out, palms facing each other, to indicate a roughly nine-inch blade and subtly lead the man to believe that he wasn't carrying another weapon. In this position, it would take Rory approximately three seconds to drop, roll and come up with the handgun in his ankle holster. Everyone in this part of Texas carried for protection against wild animals, so he assumed City Guy was armed, too.

"What makes you think it's around here?" City Guy said, keeping a cautious-looking eye on Rory while covering most of his face with the brim of his ball cap.

"According to my GPS, I was somewhere

around this area hunting this morning." He glanced at his watch. "Technically, yesterday morning. Guess it was pretty early, around daybreak." Rory was fishing to see when the guy set up camp.

"We didn't get here until noon. I checked the area as I set up and didn't see anything." The guy shrugged.

"I'm Rory, by the way."

"My name is—" there was a hesitation so brief that Rory almost wrote it off as his imagination but then City Guy finished "—Dexter but everyone calls me Dex. And this is Boots."

He made a show of scratching the dog behind his ears.

Even though Dex was considerably smaller than Rory, it was obvious the guy hit the gym. And Rory would put his life savings on the fact that the guy's name wasn't Dexter.

"Nice to meet you both." Rory picked up his earlier ruse by pretending to search the ground using his phone's flashlight app. Maybe he could needle the guy for a little information or see if he could get him talking and trip him up. "I'm such an idiot. How does someone lose a nine-inch knife?" He shook his head and threw his hands in the air.

"It most likely slipped out of your pack," Dex said. "Could happen to anyone."

"You're probably right." Rory scanned the ground. "And I'm starting to think I was crazy to think I could find anything in the dark."

"Your flashlight might catch the metal," Dex said, keeping one eye on Rory.

"That was my thought, too." If he could get the guy to think he was an amateur, he might be able to lower his defenses even more. In this case, it was hard to know who was playing whom. "You come out here a lot with Boots?"

"No. My girlfriend, Lainey, is here. We're doing a romantic thing for the night. I thought it would be a good idea. You know, the whole under-the-stars thing, but I'm not so sure she agrees. She might've ditched me and headed to a roadside motel." He laughed and it sounded a little too forced. "You didn't bump into her, did you? She'd die of embarrassment because she asked for privacy to take care of business. She's a redhead and she's wearing a white down coat, full length, with snow boots."

Dex was giving too many details as he described her. Was he nervous? Lying? There was no reason to describe his girlfriend out here. If Rory saw a woman at this hour, it would have to be her.

"Maybe I'll stick around until she gets back so I don't catch her off guard," Rory said, pretending to keep busy while waiting for a reaction.

Dex wore a red ball cap and kept his face angled toward the dog, making it difficult to make out his features, even though he was near the fire. "As long as you return the way you came, there shouldn't be a problem."

"Good point." Rory figured the more Dex believed he agreed the better. "How long are you two planning to stick around?"

Again, he listened for a slipup.

"Just the night," Dex said.

"Ah, here it is," Rory bent down and picked up something from the ground. He bit out a curse. "Never mind. It's a flattened soda can."

"Bad luck," Dex said.

"Always," Rory quipped, trying to make the guy think he was being buddy-buddy. Comradery could go a long way toward lowering Dex's defenses and getting to the truth. Why was he camping on Butler land? Rory didn't believe for one second that it was for love. This guy was here for a reason... But what?

"I better head out before your girlfriend gets

back. Wouldn't want to ruin the mood." Although, if she was really on a bathroom break, Rory couldn't imagine that was possible. But stick around much longer and Dex would become suspicious. As it was, the guy was being cautious. The campsite. The nonexistent girlfriend. The innocent camper act.

Everything was off about this situation.

"Catch you around." Rory turned and caught sight of the glint of metal in Dex's hand against the glow of the fire.

A weapon?

He decided to stick around another minute.

CADENCE BUTLER CLOSED the door to her bedroom. She was home, only it didn't feel like it since her father's murder. The place would never be the same without him. She put a hand on her growing belly as a wave of sadness crashed down around her, threatening to chew her up, toss her around and then spit her out into the surf.

Other than one quick stop over the summer, which netted an unfortunate incident with the law, she hadn't been home for good reason. Trying to scare her half sister, Madelyn, out of town had been a childish lapse in judgment. Those were racking up.

How she'd concealed her pregnancy for so long was a mystery. At six months pregnant, she was surprisingly big. Or at least she'd thought so. Her doctor had reassured her that it was perfectly normal for a woman carrying twins to show as early as she had.

Another wave of melancholy hit as she thought about the babies who would never get the chance to know their grandfather.

"I can't wait to see you running around on this land someday. Just like I used to when I was a little girl," she whispered, resting her hand on her growing baby bump.

It was late and she was grateful to have slipped inside the house without seeing anyone, without any drama. Come morning, there'd be a million questions and she still didn't know what to say about the pregnancy. Her fling with Rory had been kept secret. He'd wanted to tell her brothers but she'd convinced him not to say anything.

There was a practical reason for her coming home that didn't include the big reveal of a pregnancy with twins. She thought about the poachers encroaching on the land, taking advantage of the distractions following her father's murder. Her blood heated thinking about the kind of person who would try to capitalize on a tragedy.

Running Hereford Ranch had its challenges. Ones her father had made look so easy. But then people had known better than to mess with the ranch while her father was alive. Poachers must see the new regime, including her, as weak or they wouldn't be encroaching. They were about to be taught a valuable lesson, she thought. Her thoughts shifted to the best tracker in the country, Rory Scott. Rory was in Wyoming tracking other poachers. He'd broken her heart when he ended their fling and walked out five months ago. Thinking about it, about *him*, stressed her out.

A warm bath would do wonders toward relaxing her tension knots. Strain wasn't good for the babies. Neither was sadness and that was part of the reason she'd stayed away from the ranch. Being here without her father…

Cadence couldn't go there.

She slipped inside her room, grateful there hadn't been a big deal made over her return. No one would bother her until morning and that would give her time to think up an excuse as to why she was coming home six-months pregnant with Rory Scott's twins.

Thankfully, her bathroom was adjacent to

her room. Access was restricted. She didn't want to deal with her brothers and sister tonight. She wanted to get her bearings first. Being home, facing the ranch, brought back so many memories. Good memories that made her wish she'd had more time with her father. She gulped for air.

The father she rarely understood but always loved was never coming back.

Her heart clutched. Moving past her window, a chill raced up her spine and she got a creepy feeling. It was most likely her imagination. Or…

Was someone out there watching?

Chapter Two

"I'll be on my way before your lady friend returns. Wouldn't want to ruin the moment." Rory could see the tension building in Dex— or whatever his name was—and it was time to make his exit before this situation escalated. The glint he'd seen was most definitely from a weapon and that shot all kinds of warning flares.

Watching the campsite would be tricky with the beagle, but Rory figured he could put enough distance between them to keep off the dog's radar.

When Rory really thought about it, using a dog was smart. Dex's cover was perfect. Not many people would notice the subtle things, like the fact that the guy might be playing dumb when it came to nature, but he seemed to know enough to tie up his trash away from the site. Or that after spending a good fifteen minutes snooping around, the guy's so-called girlfriend hadn't returned. There was no alcohol on the site, either. Wouldn't that be part of a romantic camping trip for two people of drinking age? There didn't look to be any food supplies, either, which struck him as odd for someone planning to spend the night.

Was he a poacher?

Rory didn't see any of the usual supplies, consisting of water and weapons. This guy could be a scout, sending information back. This campsite was close enough to the Butler ranch that Dex might be there to watch out for ranch hands.

"Much appreciated. Camille is already skittish out here," Dex said with a wink, seemingly unaware of his mistake. Rory immediately noticed the name change. He'd called his girlfriend Lainey five minutes ago. Suddenly, her name was Camille.

Rory concealed the fact that he was scrutinizing Dex's features. The man would be fantastic at poker. For the most part, Dex kept his cards close to his chest.

"Thanks for letting me take a look around your camp." Rory offered a handshake, needing to wrap this up. He'd seen enough to know that Dex required watching. He was involved in something illegal, but there was nothing to go on besides trespassing at present. Keeping an eye on the man might lead Rory to the real source, which could be poachers. Another thought struck and that was Dex could be a reporter. Although the headlines involving the Butlers had died down a bit recently, with the will reading coming up, there'd been renewed interest in everything Butler.

"No problem." Dex stood and took the offering. The minute their palms grazed, Rory realized how nervous the guy had been. His hand had just enough moisture to reveal his emotions. Rory had to hand it to Dex, he came off as cool as a cucumber and that fact sent a few more warning flares up.

Rory walked away, careful to make sure he disappeared in the same direction he'd arrived. He could almost feel the set of eyes on his back as he walked farther from the campsite and listened carefully for any sounds that Dex might be following. He'd probably stuck around a little too long. The handshake could have been overkill. Damn.

His mistakes could lead to suspicion.

Forty-five minutes had passed since Rory recovered his previous spot, watching the campsite from afar. There'd been no movement. No Lainey, or Camille…or whatever her name was.

Rory had known that for the lie it was.

Dex tied Boots to a tree trunk. With the fire still blazing, he grabbed a walking-type stick and headed north, the opposite direction of the Butler estate.

What was he up to now?

Rory watched intently, using his night-vision goggles. He checked the time. Where did Dex think he was going at this hour?

The only evidence Rory had against the man so far was trespassing. Not exactly a strong case to entice the sheriff's office to send a deputy out immediately. The office would most likely take the complaint and promise to investigate. Sheriff Sawmill and his deputies were still too overrun to follow up on every lead unless Rory could present compelling evidence that this was more. It was hard to believe the sheriff still hadn't arrested Maverick Mike Butler's murderer.

A pang of guilt hit him like stray voltage. He'd wanted to stick around after learning that Mr. Butler had been murdered. He could only imagine the devastation the family felt and especially Cadence.

There were a few too many times in the

past five months that he'd wanted to return and be her comfort. The news coverage on Cattle Barge had almost been 24/7. He'd seen the story of her arrest and then release after she tried to run off someone claiming to be her half sister. He could only imagine what Cadence had been going through to cause a lapse in judgment like that.

Walking out five months ago had been his attempt to protect her. A relationship with Rory was the worst of bad ideas. He needed to be outside somewhere. Anywhere. And she needed a comfortable bed with soft sheets. Soft like her skin had been when he grazed his finger along the inside of her thigh.

Damn.

Thinking about Cadence brought on a surge of hormones and a wave of inappropriate desire. Hell, at least he wasn't dead. Since walking away from her, not many women could stack up to the memory of her silky skin and sweet laugh. She was beautiful and sexy, but that wasn't the best part. She was smart, and funny, and outgoing, and…

His heart clutched, squeezing a little harder this time, reminding him what a bad idea it was to think about Cadence Butler.

Being on her family's land would bring

back a certain amount of memories, he reasoned, but the onslaught of reasons why he missed her caught him off guard.

Chalk it up to weakness. Being with her had made him weak and almost forget about their differences—differences that would drive them to squabble and make each other miserable given enough time. He thought about his parents' marriage and how toxic their love had been.

Rory checked his watch again. Twenty minutes had passed while he'd been distracted by his reverie. He couldn't let that happen again.

Besides, there was no sign of Dex. He waited another full thirty minutes before making a decision on his next move. It was still too early to call the sheriff.

Patience won battles.

So, he'd hold off.

Rory waited a full hour before deciding to move closer. The dog was still secured. None of the obvious supplies had been taken. The guy's expensive-looking backpack was still leaning against his compact fold-out chair. Every sign pointed to Dex coming back.

Was he out scouting so he could relay information to his boss?

Or had he abandoned the site?

Another ten minutes wired Rory's nervous system for the unexpected. An adrenaline spike got his pulse racing and blood speeding through his veins. All his internal systems spiked to critical mass. And, like always in these situations, he felt his senses alighting, awakening. He felt alive.

He listened for any sounds that Dex was circling him, coming up from behind for a sneak attack or studying him in order to make a move. It was possible. Hell, anything was possible out here. But Dex wouldn't get the best of Rory. Rory was damn good at his job, considered the best tracker in the country.

If Dex tried to pull something, Rory would be ready and waiting.

Reaching down to his ankle holster, he pulled his Walther 9 mm and palmed it. He rested his thumb on the safety mechanism, just in case he needed to fire.

Normally, all this action and adrenaline would have boosted his mood, made him happy. Instead, a sense of dread overwhelmed him along with the energy burst. *What was that all about, Scott?*

Cadence, an irritating little voice said. Being here on her father's land. It would belong to her and her siblings now. Plus, the two surprise family members who'd shown up after Maverick Mike's death. Rory wasn't sure how either of them played into the equation but all looked to have been smoothed out based on media reports.

It's none of your business, that same little voice reminded, even though a little piece of his heart protested that everything about Cadence was.

Again, it proved nothing more than the fact that he was alive. And it was good to know that he still had a beating heart in his chest. He knew because it fisted every time he thought about her. *Having a working heart might come in handy someday*, he mused.

Although, all it had done so far was make him feel weak and angry. He thought about his family and about leaving them to run away from home at fifteen years old because he couldn't watch his parents participate in their mutual misery anymore. He'd begged his mother to leave the abuse behind, to go with him, and still couldn't understand why she'd told him to mind his own business before willingly staying with his father. The man's bouts of jealousy and anger became almost daily shows by Rory's teenage years. She'd scream and cry in the moment, threaten to leave him. Everything always escalated from there.

By the next day, always, she'd defend the man, saying that he got angry because he loved her.

A sudden burst of cold air brought his focus back to the camp twenty-five yards in front of him.

There were other possibilities for why Dex was in this part of the county, possibilities that heeded consideration. Thinking of his parents always reminded him of domestic violence. Dex could be a hothead or a common criminal in the wrong spot at the wrong time. He might've brought a girlfriend here, killed her and dug her grave. She might've already been dead and he dragged her limp body into a shallow grave.

Icy tendrils wrapped around Rory's spine at the same time that anger spiked through him.

Facing the unexpected usually kept him on his toes, reminded him he was alive. This time was surprisingly different. It lacked the excitement that normally accompanied an adrenaline rush of this scale.

Since there hadn't been activity at Dex's camp, Rory decided to go in and see if he could gather more intel. Boots was asleep and there was a chance he wouldn't bark since he'd already met Rory. The winds had picked up and the howling would mask any noise the little dog made.

What else could he use to distract the dog? Considering he didn't own a pet, nor had he ever, he didn't exactly carry around dog biscuits. Rory would have to have been willing to commit to one spot for a while in order to have his own dog. But he did have something. He could break off a small piece of a peanut-butter power bar and give it to Boots.

Dex not returning was starting to weigh on Rory. Why would the man leave the camp without taking his backpack and his pet?

Investigating could be tricky and could compromise Rory's position. What if Dex returned? What if the animal barked? Rory could be caught or shot.

Did he have another cover story? There was no good sell for being out there alone and checking out the campsite for the second time.

What if the dog didn't bark? Could Rory slip in and out without leaving a trace while Boots slept? All he'd need would be a few minutes and he was confident he could get answers.

He had to consider all possibilities.

Rory crouched low and eased across ten yards of terrain without making a sound. The howling wind played to his benefit because he could come in at an angle so the dog wouldn't easily pick up his scent. Of course, the wind chill was cutting right through his hunting jacket, which he wore in order to give off the impression he was passing through on a hunting trip. It was prime deer hunting season and that would play to his advantage. Of course, most recreational deer hunters were already locked down in a bunk on their deer lease.

Stealthily, he moved along the perimeter of the campsite.

This time, he looked for any signs that a heavy object, such as a body, had been dragged out. But then, if Dex was a murderer—and that was a big *if*—he might've already done away with the remains. The campsite could be part of his cover—girlfriend stormed off just before midnight after an intense fight. She doesn't return. Body is never found. With all the animals out searching for a meal, her remains could be scattered across the land.

It wouldn't be the first time such a tragedy had occurred. Rory had come up against similar situations and worse in his ten years as a tracker. And even though his work brought him face-to-face with everything from hardened criminals looking to hide—and willing to kill whomever stood in the way of freedom—to profiteers seeking to make a quick buck on the black market, a trade that was unfortunately thriving, to traffickers—human and animal—he'd always brought them to justice.

In his life, no two days were the same and the variety kept his blood pumping. Most of his meals were cooked and eaten out in the open. There was something about food heated over an open fire that made it taste so much better than anything he'd ever tasted from an oven.

He could admit that life on the fringe had lost some of its appeal recently and that probably had to do with the beating heart in his chest, making him think about things he knew better than to want or expect, like a real home.

This life was uncomplicated. He didn't spend his time glued to an electronic device like people in town. He didn't answer to anyone or have to spend time with anyone he didn't want to see, which also sounded lonely when he put it like that.

Taking in a slow breath, he inched forward.

Out on the range, a person's mind could wander into dangerous territory if he wasn't careful. Being alone with his thoughts for long periods used to clear his mind but not lately.

Inevitably, his thoughts would wander to Cadence. Conversations with her had always been enjoyable and especially with her spunk. Her smile was quick and genuine.

His heart acknowledged that she was dangerous and he knew deep down she could do a whole lot better in life than be dragged down by the likes of a man like him. He might've walked away first but she would've eventually. She would've figured out they were no good for each other. And his heart might not have recovered. For the hundredth time in the past five months, he reminded himself this was the only choice and that he'd done her a favor.

He'd catch the poacher who was running the show—if that man wasn't Dex—which would shut down the heart of the operation. And then get back to Wyoming, where he'd taken personal leave. He was needed on the SJ Ranch as soon as he tied up this loose end. If he was going to show his hand, he'd admit that the possibility of seeing Cadence again caused all kinds of uncomfortable feelings to surface.

For now, he'd deal with what was right in front of him, the camp. He'd managed to inch close enough to see that there was no cooler. Was Dex gone?

Rory palmed the makeshift dog treat. Improvising was the name of the game out in the wild, where he'd learned to make do with what was on hand.

Boots opened his eyes and lifted his head as Rory dropped down next to him. Rory was no dog whisperer but he knew his way around animals. Another survival tactic. One he enjoyed.

"Shhhh, it's okay, Boots." He held out the broken pieces of power bar on his flat palm as he surveyed the area. Dex could show up any minute.

And then his gaze landed on the object that Dex had been hiding…a rifle with a scope pointing south, the direction of the Butler home.

Hold on. From this vantage point on the land, could he see as far as the estate? It would depend on the power of the scope.

Rory emptied his hand of the treats, dropping them next to the dog's mouth. Boots wagged his tail as he happily went to town on the bits.

Rory pulled his night goggles down from his forehead and secured them over his eyes. Another quick scan of the area and everything looked copacetic. Of course, the goggles only allowed him to see fifteen feet around. Pitch-blackness circled the camp like a heavy fog.

He gave another pass to the area in order to make sure he and Boots were alone.

Dropping down to check the angle of the scope, he removed his goggles.

A curse rolled up and out.

Dex had a perfect angle.

The rifle was aimed at the Butler estate all right.

Rory would recognize that bedroom window anywhere.

It belonged to Cadence Butler.

Chapter Three

Rory backed away, making sure he didn't damage any of the fingerprints on the rifle or scope, and then he called the sheriff.

"There's a situation on the Butler property you need to be aware of," he said to Sheriff Sawmill. Rory could almost see the frustration that accompanied the heavy sigh coming through the line. "I can give you my GPS coordinates."

"Mind sending a few photos of the site?" Sawmill asked.

"Not if it'll help," Rory said. He didn't mind taking a few risks if it meant helping Sawmill figure out who Dex really was.

"I don't have anyone near your location. I'll get a deputy out before morning," he promised.

"Thanks, Sheriff." There was no use pressuring him. Rory could tell by the man's tone that he wished he could do more but didn't have the resources. He also knew how overstretched the sheriff's office had been since the murder. Pressure mounted to find Mr. Butler's killer as time went on and that had to be weighing on the sheriff's mind.

After snapping pictures from multiple angles and then watching over the site for another half hour, Rory assumed Dex wasn't coming back. The most likely scenario was that Rory had scared Dex away and he wouldn't return. The man had taken off in a hurry after Rory had invaded the camp and the probability there'd be fingerprints on the weapon were slim to none.

The fire had burned out. Since Rory couldn't rightly leave the little dog to freeze, he took the shivering beagle into his arms and placed him inside his jacket so he would stop shaking.

Dex would know someone had been there if he returned before the sheriff's deputy arrived. Rory highly doubted the guy was coming back, though, based on experience.

Game on, Rory thought as he tracked east. He'd circle around to his conversion vehicle and take the beagle, which couldn't be more than a year old, with no tags, with him to the

Butler ranch. If Dex thought he could out-smart him, he needed to think again. No one was better out on the range than Rory and he had no doubt that he could track Dex and see to it that the guy spent the rest of his life behind bars.

Cadence was home. Rory wasn't supposed to know that. No one was. However, he couldn't help himself and had tracked her whereabouts. She'd left Colorado that evening and would've arrived an hour or two ago. He needed to warn her and her family that she could be in danger.

A dark thought hit. Had Dex already made his way to the main house?

That thought had Rory picking up the pace. In a full-out run, Rory made it back to his vehicle in record time. He secured the beagle in the front seat and took the driver's seat before heading southwest toward the main house. From his current location, it would take an hour to wind around on the country roads to get to the place. He knew a shortcut that involved going off road but could possibly get a lot of attention from security.

Rory spun the wheel left. He needed to get to the house as fast as possible. It was possible that Dex had moved closer to get a good shot. Damn. The man might've left his rifle behind but he was still carrying a handgun.

It was also worth considering that he was an amateur and had abandoned his plan altogether.

Rory managed to locate his phone while driving and used Bluetooth technology to make the call to Cadence.

The recording said the number was no longer in service.

When did she change her number? She'd had the same one since high school.

Then he thought about everything that had happened to the family in the past few months after Maverick Mike Butler's death. With all the media scrutiny, it made sense that she would make it more difficult to reach her. He hoped it had to do with the media and not their breakup. It shouldn't bother him that she'd changed her number. It wasn't really his business anymore no matter how much his heart argued.

Okay. Plan B.

He pulled over and checked his call log. Dade had been the one to reach out, so his new number must be on the log. Rory called that number. He didn't realize he'd been holding his breath until the call rolled into a generic-sounding voice mail and frustration nipped at him.

Instead, he tapped the gas pedal harder and raced toward the house, hoping like hell that he wasn't too late.

Someone in the Butler household knew there'd been a security breach because Terrell Landry stood with his rifle shouldered and aimed at the conversion vehicle speeding toward the back side of the estate. Based on his disposition, his finger hovered over the trigger mechanism. A team of six formed a semicircle around Terrell twenty yards in front of where Rory stopped the conversion vehicle and put his hands where everyone could see them as he exited his vehicle. He'd be no use to Cadence or anyone else if he got himself shot on the property and he wouldn't risk one of the men he didn't know getting too excited with his trigger finger.

"Rory Scott?" Terrell said, more statement than question.

"In the flesh," Rory answered. "Permission to approach?"

Terrell's next words allowed Rory to exhale.

"Of course. Stand down," Terrell told his men, lowering his own weapon. "But what are you doing here? I was told that you refused the job."

"Misunderstanding," Rory said as he walked to the head of security, planning to meet him halfway. He'd known Terrell for half of his life.

"Good to see you," Terrell said, sticking out his hand between them.

Rory shook it as the others flanked them. And then a few seconds later he found himself flipped on his backside, heaving for air after being slammed into the cold hard pavement with the wind knocked out of him.

"What the hell, Landry?" he managed to get out through gulps of air. His lungs burned.

"I'm sorry, Rory. I have orders," Terrell said. "I've been instructed to contain you and call the sheriff in order to file a trespassing complaint."

"The Butlers offered me a job. Who would give you orders to have me arrested?" Rory ground out.

"I got the order directly from Cadence Butler." He shot another apologetic look. "She called it in yesterday."

She had to know that Rory would have been asked to help. Yes, he'd walked out on a relationship with her but this was over the top. Even for Cadence.

Twenty minutes later, Rory stood in the foyer of the Butler home with his hands in zip cuffs and Boots at his side.

Dade came rushing toward him as Boots sat next to Rory's shoes. "I'm sorry, Rory. I don't know how this order slipped past the rest of us and ended up being issued. It should never have happened." He glanced toward his head of security and then the zip cuffs. "Take those ridiculous things off."

Rory's anger almost overshadowed the real reason he'd shown up to begin with as Terrell removed the bindings. He rubbed sore wrists. "I caught a guy on your property with a scope on Cadence's room."

Dalton entered the foyer, stress cracks around his eyes and mouth. He looked exhausted and Rory didn't like being the one to deliver more bad news. "Where?"

"Due north from the main house," Rory supplied. "Is she here?"

"Haven't seen her yet but she was due in last night," Dade supplied after shaking his friend's hand. Dade was wearing jeans without a shirt or shoes. He'd obviously been roused from sleep. "I'm sorry again for the misunderstanding." He motioned toward Rory's wrists.

This was no miscommunication, but he wasn't angry at Dade or Dalton for it.

"You want me to take care of this guy?" Landry asked, motioning toward Boots.

"He belong to you?" Dade asked.

"Does now."

"All right if Landry takes care of him while we talk?" Dade nodded toward the beagle.

"Fine by me. Cadence needs to know how much danger she's in." She wasn't stupid and if she realized how close she was to being shot, she'd take the right precautions. Rory didn't even want to think about what might've happened if he hadn't been there. Was he still frustrated with her for the stunt? Hell, yes.

But he didn't want anything to happen to her.

It was probably guilt for walking out on her that had him wanting to protect her and not residual feelings. Rory didn't *do* those with anyone no matter how much his heart wanted to argue at thinking about seeing her again.

"I need to talk to Cadence," Rory said as Landry picked up Boots and then disappeared.

Dade stepped aside, allowing access to her hallway in the massive rustic-chic, log-cabin-style home. It looked more like a resort than private residence and he knew the layout well.

"She doesn't want to talk to you." Ella Butler stepped into the hallway in front of Cadence's room.

"Too bad," Rory said. "She needs to."

Ella was shaking her head and she looked rattled by the ordeal. "We understand what happened and will take it seriously. My sister has nothing else to say to you."

"Like hell she doesn't." He started toward her room.

Ella stood there, arms folded over her chest. He would never do anything to hurt a woman so he flexed and released his fingers to keep them from reaching out to pick her up and move her.

"What's going on?" Dade's brow was hiked.

"Good question," Rory added, focusing on Ella. "Your sister can have me arrested if I set foot on the property when I've been summoned, but I don't get to warn of her the danger she's in or ask why she's so intent on not seeing me?"

"No, you don't. Now, leave," Cadence said from her room.

"This is none of our business, Ella," Dade

warned and Rory wondered if his friend knew about the fling. He doubted it, considering how determined Cadence had been to keep it under wraps.

Just when Rory thought Ella was going to dig her heels in and fight, her expression softened and she said, "You're right. We should stay out of it. I'm sorry, Cadence. But he deserves to know."

Cadence didn't respond.

"I'm sorry, Rory," Ella said with a look as she, Dalton and Dade wished him good luck before disappearing down the hall.

Deserved to know what exactly? Rory questioned.

Rory tapped on Cadence's door with his bare knuckles. He was the one who'd said there was no future for the two of them and then taken a job in Wyoming. When he really thought about it, she had every right to be upset with him. Not to trust him. Having him detained for being on Butler land was going too far but Cadence had a flair for the dramatic and she was probably still acting out of hurt—hurt that had been his fault.

"It's important or I wouldn't be here, Cadence. Open up," he said.

"Go away."

CADENCE STOOD ON the opposite side of the door, her heart thundering in her chest. This wasn't how she'd envisioned telling Rory that he was going to be a father. She'd had every intention of telling him when the time was right but that time never came and she'd eventually decided to wait until after the babies were born.

There'd been so many times she'd wanted him to know but to what end? What did she want from him? Child support? Marriage? She almost laughed out loud at the thought of tying Rory down with commitment. He'd been all too clear that he wasn't the type to stick around.

When he'd first walked out of her life, she thought that if she gave him enough time, he'd come back on his own. He'd realize that the two of them should be together.

As far as drinking the Kool-Aid went, she'd gone all-in with that fantasy.

He'd seemed content to stay away and her heart was still trying to heal from the snub.

So far, Ella was the only one who knew about the pregnancy and her sister had literally found out five minutes ago when she'd come in to check on Cadence.

"Stay away from your windows, Cadence.

Someone was camping on your property and you're being targeted." Rory wasn't trying to scare her. His voice was steady steel.

"Okay. Now I know," she retorted, chiding herself for being so quick to dismiss him.

Several more taps came.

"I'm sorry about what happened between us." His voice was low and gravelly. It was the same voice that had been so good at seducing her.

And the same that had told her the two of you didn't have a future, a little voice reminded.

"Fine. I'll take this seriously. Consider me warned. Now, you can leave." He deserved to know he was a father but not like this. A cramp nearly doubled her over. She made it to her bed and sat down, gripping the mattress, trying not to make a noise.

She'd sent for a doctor four times in her first trimester, thinking the cramps were a bad sign that something was going terribly wrong. Turned out they were normal and especially common in a first pregnancy.

Before she could stop it, the doorknob twisted.

"No, Rory! Go!"

"I just wanted to tell you face-to-face—"

His jaw fell slack the minute his gaze landed on her stomach.

Defensively, she brought her hands around her large belly to cover it.

Rory stood there, frozen, as though unable to speak.

A few seconds ticked by before he seemed to gather his thoughts well enough to say something.

"Do you mind telling me when you intended to share the news that you're pregnant?" he finally asked, and there was so much betrayal in his voice.

She was pretty sure he was decent at math but also certain he had no idea how far along she was or the timing of a pregnancy. And part of her realized he had every right to be angry.

"I'd say it's none of your business but that's not exactly true since you're the father," she said, watching intently for his response.

A look of complete shock darkened his features as his gaze practically bore through her. His jaw clenched and released a few times, and it looked like he was grinding his molars. His stare became a dare when he said, "Then marry me."

Chapter Four

"For what reason, Rory Scott?" There was a time when Cadence would've said yes in a heartbeat to a marriage proposal from Rory. But this one had the stench of obligation attached to it and from the sounds of it, anger. Just how well would that work out for her or the babies?

She'd seen firsthand the problems with that logic. Her father had married her mother because she'd been pregnant with Cadence's older sister. Her mother had apparently been so miserable that she'd taken off when Cadence was still in diapers.

"You're pregnant for one. It's what a man does," he stated, squaring his shoulders.

"We're done with this conversation," Cadence said, covering the hurt. His words were knife jabs to her chest. Because a part of her she didn't want to acknowledge still had feelings for him. A whole lot of good that did. Of course, she cared about Rory. He was the father of her growing babies.

"No, we're not anything, Cadence. You can't run away from this." His words had the effect of bullets from a machine gun, slamming into the target wildly and with inaccuracy.

"Why don't you just leave again? Take off. You know you want to," she shot back. The two of them were just as opposite as they had been when he'd broken off their fling and taken off five months ago. Nothing had changed. Neither one of them was different. Okay, that part wasn't exactly true or fair. Cadence was different. She put her hands protectively around her belly. "It must feel awfully hot in here to you."

"You're trying to make it that way." He had a lot of nerve blaming her.

"I'm sorry that you're finding out this way. This is not what I had planned. None of this was on my agenda, actually. But the only thing a pregnancy does is make us parents, Rory." She blew out a breath. This wasn't the way she'd intended for him to find out and emotions were already running too high. Someone needed to have some common sense, and they both needed to cool it for a minute before her blood pressure careened out of control. "I need a drink."

He shot her a look that dared her to have a glass of wine.

"Of water." She stormed past him, needing to break the bad energy in the room. She stomped down the hallway, into the kitchen, and stopped in front of the fridge after grabbing a glass from the counter. She filled it while he made himself at home with the coffeepot. And then she whirled around on him. "What are you really doing here, Rory? I know you didn't come to see me."

"You're in danger," he said.

"That's not answering my question," she shot back. "You couldn't have known that until you arrived."

"Your brother called and offered me a job. I need the money," he said.

Dalton and Dade walked into the kitchen, both stopped and stared at Cadence.

"I'm pregnant," she said to her twin brothers, watching as their jaws fell slack.

"Hold on a second," Dade said, looking like he was trying to absorb the news. It also seemed to dawn on him that this was the reason she'd objected to their calling in Rory for the job.

"You two?" Dade looked from Cadence to Rory and she was pretty sure she saw a look pass between her brother and Rory. Shock? Anger? Betrayal?

This was exactly the reason she'd wanted to keep their fling quiet. She hadn't needed her brothers weighing in on her love life and they'd been close with Rory growing up. He'd wanted to tell them but she'd known better than to clue them in. Seeing the look of guilt on Rory's face now had her questioning her judgment.

"I didn't know anything about the pregnancy until ten minutes ago but I take full responsibility," Rory said with a look of apology toward her brothers. He was trying to do the right thing by her and she could appreciate the act of honor. She was also realistic enough to know that a forced marriage wouldn't make either one of them happy; she'd seen what could happen when two people had children who didn't love each other. "I asked her to marry me but she turned me down."

"Why would you do that?" Dalton asked Cadence.

"My personal life is off-limits to you and

you." She pointed her finger at each brother individually in case they didn't get it that she was talking about both of them.

Dade started to argue but Dalton stopped him with a hand up.

"We have a bigger issue to deal with right now," Dalton said.

Ella joined them with an awkward look at Cadence's bump. What was that all about? She knew her sister wasn't making a moral judgment. Dalton was right. There was another pressing problem to address.

"My family filled me in on what's happening on the land with poachers. I get that someone's on the land that we need to get rid of but I thought you didn't want the job," she said to Rory.

"Not *you* as in the family. I mean *you* as in," he motioned toward her with his hands. "*You* personally."

"What happened?" Dalton said as her brothers closed ranks around her. "And she's right. You refused the job. So what are you doing here?" There was more than a hint of aggravation in his voice. Again, Cadence would deal with her family later. This was exactly the reason she didn't want to be in Cattle Barge in the first place. Her siblings had always acted more like parents to her and she was a grown woman.

"I thought it would be best if no one knew I was working or in the area. That's the reason I refused the job. I had every intention of helping, paid or not. I hope you know I'd do whatever it took if any one of you needed me." He had a long history with the family and was the same age as the twins. As their little sister, she'd trailed behind on their adventures, wanting to be included, but she had been so young. She had known Rory and vice versa for ages and that was exactly the reason Cadence knew a real relationship with Rory would never work. He craved independence a little too much to be tethered by a family of his own. She'd known it from the beginning and that was probably half the fun of spending time with him. He was untamed and untamable much like the land. There was a certain beauty to that freedom, which she admired.

Just like a too-wild horse, putting a saddle on it broke its spirit. She didn't have the heart to do that to Rory.

Cadence had always been drawn to a challenge. She couldn't regret the pregnancy, not since she felt her children's first movements, but that didn't mean the situation wasn't complicated. But losing her father and the subsequent attacks on her siblings had given her a new respect for how quickly everything could be taken away from her. She was learning to appreciate every day and embrace the adventures life brought.

Rory stood there in the family kitchen and she couldn't deny that he still looked good—damn good. It was probably hormones making her weak, making her notice the sexy dark stubble on his chin. He'd always had rugged good looks and she'd tried to forget how handsome he was. Dark hair, dark eyes. He was intense. About everything. Including making love. Especially making love.

A trill of awareness skittered across her skin at the memories.

Lot of good thinking about that would do.

She tuned back in as he was explaining the campsite he'd come upon. There was an animal, a beagle, which he'd brought with him and was now in the sleeping quarters with the ranch hands.

"Why is he out there and not in here?" Cadence asked a little too forcefully.

"I have no idea if Boots is housebroken and I couldn't leave the poor thing alone on the land with all the coyotes," Rory said.

"I wasn't suggesting you should leave him out there." She swept her hand toward the backyard.

Rory started to speak but cocked his head to the side and compressed his lips.

"The rifle was trained on the house and when I checked the scope it was aimed at Cadence's window," he said, glancing at the open shutter. He moved to the double doors that led to the patio and started closing blinds.

Dalton smacked his flat palm against the counter and grunted a swear word before joining Rory.

"It would be a tough shot but it's possible with a high-powered rifle," Dade said after a thoughtful silence. He muttered a few choice words under his breath as he worked to close the blinds in the great room.

Ella stared at the granite countertop. "We need to let security know what's going on. They'll want to take action against the threat."

"Good idea. But keep in mind a trained shooter can hit a target from quite a distance and Landry didn't find the guy. I did," Rory supplied. "A professional would know to account for wind and velocity as well as other variables, even with a difficult shot."

"We need to call the sheriff," Ella said.

"Already did."

"How about the guy? Did you get a good look at him?" Cadence asked. The horror of what was going on started sinking in.

"Yes." He provided a description. "Do you know who he is?"

"Not off the top of my head." Cadence searched her brain. Surely, she'd seen the guy before.

"Which means Cadence doesn't go anywhere," Dalton said with a look toward her. "Agreed?"

"Are we sure someone is after *me*?" She couldn't fathom the thought, even though, to be fair, several of her siblings had been targeted since their father's death. With the reading of the will coming up, everything could be stirring up again.

"I can't think of who would want to hurt you but I'm giving Terrell the description of him so he can alert the others and keep watch for the guy," Ella said. She was already texting.

"I'm guessing that you're limiting access to the ranch based on recent events," Rory said.

"That's right," Ella supplied.

It was probably just because she needed to eat but Cadence was dizzy and felt a bout of nausea coming on. This couldn't be right. She'd been in Colorado for months now and had hoped to return the minute the will was read. This definitely wasn't the time to tell her family that she had plans to move to Colorado on a permanent basis but Cattle Barge was proving to be unsafe for a Butler. She realized she'd been touching her stomach without noticing it. The move was becoming habit. She was already attached to the little people inside. "I'm not saying that we shouldn't take every precaution but the wind could've moved the gun. I mean, it's cold and windy outside and I don't even think anyone knows I'm home."

"Good. Let's keep it that way. Maybe this guy was aiming at a random room and it had nothing to do with you personally," Rory offered. There was enough hope in his voice to make Cadence believe he still cared about her. At least in general terms, and he probably cared even more now that he knew she was pregnant with his child. This didn't seem like the time to tell him she was having twins.

He might've made it clear that he wasn't the settling-down or parenting type when she'd thrown caution to the wind and had the fling she'd craved—or was it excitement? Who could tell anymore? Point being, he didn't want the responsibility of a family and she hadn't planned on any of this happening, either. There they were. Stuck in a situation and now it seemed that her life was on the line.

"WHAT KIND OF rifle did you say he had?" Dalton asked.

"M40." One look at Cadence—at the hurt Rory had caused her—was all it took for him to know Maverick Mike Butler had been right. Rory was bad for Cadence. The senior Butler had given Rory a job on the ranch when he was destitute with the condition that Rory stayed away from his daughter. He must've seen the way Rory had looked at Cadence then. He'd given his word—and that was all he had to give at the time because he was poor—that he'd leave her alone. As soon as he came to his senses during their fling, realizing that Cadence would always be a Butler and he would never be the man she needed him to be, he'd done what he should've long ago and cut her loose.

At the time, she'd told him it was fine with her. She'd been convincing and he'd believed her. Until now. Until he saw the hurt deep in her eyes that she was trying to cover with anger. Until he realized she was hurting because of his rejection.

She could literally have any man she wanted. If Rory lived to be a hundred and ten years old he wouldn't understand her. Her express rejection of his marriage proposal had him scratching his head and more than a little offended. He knew he was broken, but did she have to rebuke his offer so fast? Did she have to cut him down so quickly? He also couldn't understand why she didn't seem to want protection and especially while she was in such a fragile state. He almost laughed out loud. Cadence fragile? Pregnant or not, she'd always been a firecracker. Although, judging from the looks of her determination and everything he already knew about her, she didn't seem at a disadvantage in any way shape or form, no matter the obstacle.

In fact, she seemed like even more of a force to be reckoned with now that she was carrying a child. *His child.* The fact that he was going to have a baby hadn't really absorbed yet. Maybe when this whole scenario was over and the Butlers were out of danger, he could consider what was going on. Laser focus and the ability to shut everything else out had kept him alive so far.

Besides, how could he feel good about bringing a little person into the world with his messed-up background? His parents were the epitome of explosives and an agitator. Those two fought like cats and dogs, if cats and dogs were venomous creatures. The only person he'd been close to growing up had been his sister and he hadn't seen her since he was fifteen. She'd taken off the minute she'd turned seventeen and never looked back. Back then, there was very little social media and Rory wasn't the type to be online anyway. Hell, he still wasn't. His smartphone didn't even have email loaded. It had the capability but he'd never felt like he needed to be reached that badly.

Dade and Dalton had been like brothers. Rory had been friends with the Butler twins, Cadence's brothers, since they were all knee-high, and being close to a tight-knit family—at least from the perimeter—had been one of the best experiences. It had almost given him hope that he could have that someday, too. And that thinking was what had gotten him into bed with Cadence in the first place. It was also the line of thinking that had had him imagining everything would magically work out.

Wishing was for kids with quarters standing in front of fountains.

The look of betrayal in Dade's and Dalton's eyes was a knife to the chest. Rory deserved it.

He clued back into the conversation going on around him when he heard the words *it could be the same.*

"I mean, the guy, or person, who shot our father had the same kind of rifle," Ella said.

"It's one of the most popular rifles around." Rory didn't say that it was popular with criminals.

"But we can't rule it out," Ella continued.

"Not without a ballistics report," Dalton interjected.

Ella locked eyes with her sister. "Don't take this the wrong way, but have you pulled any of your stunts lately?"

Cadence folded her arms across her chest. "Do I look capable of doing anything besides eating and sleeping?"

Ella turned to Rory after another quick glance at her sister. "I'm sorry about what happened to you earlier with our security."

His hands were already up to stop her before she could say anything else. "You have to be careful and no one expected me."

"We didn't suspect you of anything. You know that, right?" she continued.

"Of course not."

"Then will you stay on?" Ella asked. Cadence grunted.

"And where will I go?" she asked.

"Right here." Ella must've caught on to the fight she was about to get from her younger sister because she threw her hands up. "I realize the plan is not without complications. But now that security has seen Rory and presumably the man who wants one or all of us dead has, too, we need all the extra help we can get around here."

Cadence started to speak but Ella shot her a severe look.

"Our dad's will is going to be read in five days and the town is already starting to work itself into a frenzy about a big revelation in the will. Maybe the guy who aimed a gun at this house has something to lose," Ella continued. She moved toward the coffee machine. "I doubt I'll sleep tonight and work is good for feeling anxious. I'll throw on a fresh pot. Is anyone hungry? I could cook something—"

"I appreciate the offer but I'm better off sleeping out there." Rory motioned toward the ranch hands' bunkhouse. He didn't feel right sleeping in Maverick Mike's house, knowing that the man wouldn't want him there. It seemed wrong and that might be twisted logic considering Cadence was pregnant. But Maverick Mike was gone and Rory wanted to respect the man's wishes as if he were still alive.

"No way," Ella protested.

Cadence issued another grunt and her frustration shouldn't have made him want to chuckle. He suppressed the urge, figuring he'd only make matters worse.

"At least stick around long enough to help us come up with a plan," Ella said.

Rory noticed that Dade and Dalton had been mostly quiet so far. They had to realize he'd had no idea about the pregnancy. But he'd betrayed their friendship by not telling them about his relationship with their sister.

When they were young, Cadence had been the annoying little sister. Dade and Dalton had refused to let her hang around. If they had, Rory might've viewed her like a younger sister, too. He'd felt a brotherhood with the twins that hadn't extended to Ella and Cadence since he hadn't been close with the girls. Mr. Butler had made damn sure his daughters hadn't had anything to do with the hired hands. But the boys had been like brothers. More guilt nipped at him thinking about it.

And then there was Cadence.

She sure as hell didn't seem to want him underfoot based on the way she stood there alternating between touching the growing bump and fisting her hands at her sides when she looked at him. Did she realize how much danger she was in? Did she know he had no plans to leave until she was safe?

The idea of becoming a father crashed down on him while looking at her.

Dammit, she looked even more beautiful.

"If I'm the target and it's only me this person is after, doesn't it make more sense for me to leave the ranch so everyone else will be safe?" Cadence asked after a thoughtful pause. "What if he confuses me for Ella and she accidentally gets shot in my place. I'd never be able to forgive myself if a bullet meant for me hit her."

Ella swiped at a tear, clearly getting emotional over her sister's revelation. "That's not going to happen."

Even so, Cadence had a point. Plus, security had been compromised on the ranch. The place wasn't set up for attacks on the Butlers. Poachers, yes. And there was general security

at the main house. The guard shack in front
and foot patrols kept away the kinds of threats
they normally faced. But there'd been several
attempts on Butlers in recent months and although thankfully everything had worked out,
that didn't mean their luck would hold. Mr.
Butler had been murdered on the ranch and
the killer had been crafty enough to get away
with it so far.

Looking at Cadence, it was clear to Rory
that she had an idea of just how much danger
she was in. Although, she looked to be taking
everything in and considering possibilities.

"Where would you go?" he asked her.

"I'd be safer anywhere but here in Cattle
Barge, where everyone knows our business
and every move we make." It was clear that
she was building up to something.

"What did you have in mind? Europe?"
Getting her as far away from the ranch as
possible didn't sound like the worst possible
idea. Especially if it meant he could keep her
out of the line of fire until he figured this out.

"I was thinking more like Colorado," she
said.

"Why would that be safe?"

"Correct me if I'm wrong but I've already
been there for months, ever since Dad…" Her

voice broke. "And no one has tried to do anything to me so far. It's clearly safer for me there, which also raises the question, if this person was after me in the first place, why come here?"

More good points.

"I'll give you that the person might not've known you'd be coming home. Maybe he was watching until you did," Rory argued. "There's something to be said about going back to Colorado and possibly being safer, except that it would be easy to follow you now that he's found you. I don't think it's worth it to travel all the way there. But believe me, this is a win in his mind even if I threw off his immediate plans. He knows where you are. Could he have known when to expect you?"

"I doubt it," Cadence said.

"Have there been any new hires on the ranch recently? Anyone who could've tipped this guy off?" Rory continued.

"No one knew I was coming home except for my family, our lawyer and May," Cadence supplied. "I trust every one of those people with my life."

"Agreed," Rory said. The family lawyer, Ed Staples, was like an uncle to the Butler siblings and May, the housekeeper, had been a surrogate mother.

Rory needed to think. He paced around the kitchen.

"We could let this guy know where you'd be," he said.

"Why would we do that?" Ella quipped.

"Let him finish," Dalton said. It was the first sign of support since the news of his relationship with Cadence had been revealed earlier.

"Maybe there's a way to make a big deal out of pretending you've come home. Set up a time and place the guy thinks you'll be somewhere while I sneak you away from the ranch."

"We could throw a baby shower," Ella interjected. "Pretend that you're here and it's happening tomorrow."

"That's a solid possibility," Dalton offered. "Word travels fast in Cattle Barge."

"How soon can I leave?" Cadence asked.

"Out of an abundance of caution, you should go soon," Ella said. "If someone's trying to get to you, I don't want to risk your life or add strain to the pregnancy."

Dade, who had been quiet up until now,

stepped forward. "The only way I'll agree to this is if Rory goes with her."

"Hold on a minute," Cadence defended. "I'm old enough to make my own decisions and I don't need the family to—"

"I know you won't put you or your child's life in danger by rejecting help," Dade said sternly. And Rory could almost see the hairs on Cadence's neck stand on end.

She was gearing up for battle and the stress couldn't be good for her or the baby she was carrying. He needed to have a serious sit down with her once this storm blew over and figure a few things out, but for now, he needed to find a way to keep her calm.

"If she's good with me helping, I'm all in. I'm more than willing to offer assistance but not without her agreement," Rory said, although he fully believed that he had every right to make sure his child and its mother were safe. "The last thing she needs is more stress and I've already caused enough by showing up."

She stared him down like a prizefighter from across the ring. Her arched brow gave away that she was trying to figure out his game. He didn't have one. All he wanted was for Cadence to be safe and he was the best man for the job.

"I'm leaving," Cadence stated. "I'm perfectly capable of taking care of myself and the last thing I need is a babysitter."

Surely, there was some way to change her mind. Looking at her right then with her determined gaze and jutted chin, Rory feared there wasn't.

"Forget it. She's too stubborn," he said.

Chapter Five

To Cadence, this situation was no different than the time Dade and Dalton had stepped in between her and Granger Peabody on the playground. Standing up for her was fine, appreciated even, but they'd steamrollered right over Granger when the two of them were only playing and hadn't listened to her when she'd tried to reason with them to let them know he wasn't hurting her. The two had been playing Damsel in Distress and he was the villain.

Granger had been a friend until her brothers warned him to stay away or else. The ten-year-old boy wouldn't have anything to do with her after that and it had been a lonely rest of the year. Fifth grade had spiraled into sixth when the twins had knocked the tooth out of the first boy who'd kissed her.

Granted, he hadn't had permission but she'd been prepared to stand up for herself and not look like someone who couldn't take care of herself.

Instead of being her saviors, they'd turned into her worst nightmares. Because of them she'd been teased her entire life for not being able to fight her own battles. That was one of the many reasons she wanted to live in Colorado and not Texas. Her heart would always be with the land and her family roots but no one felt the need to stand up for her in Colorado. She was free to live without the burden of the family name. And, yes, Maverick Mike Butler's name—and reputation—certainly traveled with her, but he was too big for life in Texas, making it impossible to step out of his shadow.

Her brothers were too overbearing here and she could only imagine how much more protective they'd be of her babies. Especially since she'd be bringing them up on her own.

When she was on her first date, both of her brothers had shown up at the movies and sat on either side of her and Rickie Hampton. Exactly what did they think she was going to be doing in public at the theater on Main Street? Kiss? It had been bad enough that Rickie had had to go through a security gate in order to pick her up. Talk about the death of a social life. Everyone believed the Butlers thought they had their noses in the air anyway and she guessed their sticking together hadn't helped much. No amount of Ella's volunteering had made a hill of beans difference. People thought what they wanted despite all evidence to the contrary.

Cadence had learned that lesson the hard way. The few friends she'd made had been using her, believing there'd be some kind of benefit to being a Butler friend. School had been lonely. Dade and Dalton had had each other. She knew the twins and Ella loved her, but smothering her wasn't the same as being close.

To Cadence, having her family following her every move—well intentioned as it might've been—had been suffocating. Madelyn and Wyatt were welcomed additions now that Madelyn had forgiven Cadence for her childish behavior when her newfound sister had first come to town after being summoned by the family lawyer.

"There's just one problem with our plan," she finally said.

"And that is?" Ella asked.

"No one is going to believe a baby shower being set up in a few hours," Cadence said.

Rory nodded. "He'll see right through that."

"There's something else we could use, though," Cadence said. "The will." She referred to the stipulation that it be read on Christmas Eve with the entire family present.

"If all of you are in the same place at the same time it'll be easy to strike and take down more than just Cadence," Rory said.

Ella paced as the twins nodded in agreement.

"How about this?" Ella finally broke through the quiet of the last few minutes. "What if we send out word that the will is going to be read tomorrow night instead?" She checked the clock on the wall. "Make that tonight."

"Is there time to set that up?" Cadence asked.

"We'll let it leak online and then it'll get picked up as gospel. We all already know everything we say and do gets reported," she said, looking to her brothers and then Ella. "Even when it's wrong."

Dade's eyes perked up. "It could work. Tell the right source. Set up a fake meet up and see what happens."

"Cadence would be far away," Rory interjected.

"But no one has to know that," Ella said.

Cadence had to admit the idea might just work. The faster the sheriff caught the man targeting someone in the family—her?—the quicker she could come clean about her future plans to her siblings. She might have a temper and make decisions she sometimes regretted after acting in the moment, but she wasn't a liar. Keeping secrets from the family didn't feel right. Everything they'd been through since losing their father had made them even closer. *Father.* She couldn't even think about him without a lump forming in her throat. What would he have thought about twin baby girls for grandchildren? She rubbed her belly again without thinking about it.

Although Maverick Mike Butler had a wild streak a mile long, he'd become more even keeled as he aged. Getting older had been nice on him. He'd worn his years well and seemed to settle into his personality more. Like there was more softness about him and less to prove. He'd confided in her that he had an announcement to make to the family. She'd suspected he was going to tell everyone that he wasn't going to be a bachelor much longer.

Her idea to move to Colorado permanently had hit her after talking to her father. Give him and the rest of the gang at Cattle Barge up and make a life for herself in Colorado. She wished she'd told her father about her plans. Was it weird that she still wished for his approval?

"If this is going to work we need to get Ed Staples involved," Ella said, pacing around the kitchen island.

"True," she said.

Dade stood at the island while Dalton put on another pot of coffee.

"Let's start planning." Dade pulled his phone from his pocket and set it on the counter. "Now, who should we tell in order to spread the word fastest?"

"That's easy," Ella said. "We'll start with the *NewsNow!* reporter, Cameron-something, who's been hiding inside almost every bush I've walked past for months on end."

"Won't he question suddenly having a real story fall in his lap?" Dade asked.

"I doubt it," Ella said on a sharp sigh. "He's hungry for any piece of information he can get on us. He won't question the source, especially when the information will come from a Butler."

Dalton rocked his head in agreement, a look of disdain darkening his features.

"We haven't talked about this yet, but is

there anyone you can think of who would want to scare you, Cadence?" Dalton poured a cup of coffee for himself and offered one to Rory.

"No," she admitted as Rory took the cup from her brother. She really was clueless as to who would want to hurt her. "I haven't even been in Cattle Barge since Dad's murder and I kept a low profile in Colorado. I doubt anyone could've tracked me there."

Rory issued a grunt noise.

"What's that supposed to mean?" She whirled around on him.

"I knew where you were and when you left," he said, and then it seemed to dawn on him that he'd revealed he'd been watching her.

"How good can you be at your job, Rory? You didn't even know I was carrying your child." She regretted the insult as soon as she hurled it. "Look, I didn't mean that. I'm just saying—"

It was too late. Rory had already stalked out back and slammed the door behind him.

"I WASN'T TRYING to upset you," Cadence called after Rory, stopping him in his tracks.

He immediately backpedaled as he glanced around. It was pitch-black outside save for the light above the barn door and another at the back porch. "Are you crazy or just trying to put yourself in harm's way?"

"What?" A look of confusion knitted her brows.

"Anyone could be hiding in the tree line. Get back inside, Cadence."

She looked like she was about to mount an argument but then her gaze darted around toward the darkened areas of the yard. Much to his surprise, she turned tail and headed back inside. He followed her.

The kitchen had cleared out, which was good. He didn't want to say what he had to in front of her siblings no matter how close he was to her brothers.

"A lot has happened and you should probably think about getting some rest," he started and before she could become indignant, he held up his hands in surrender and said, "I'm not telling you what to do. Do what you want. It's a suggestion."

Her heart-shaped lips bowed. "I didn't take it the wrong way." She stopped short of saying *this time*. But he'd take it. At least she didn't look ready to hurl a coffee cup at him. He'd call that progress.

He'd also seize on the good will.

"I don't want you anywhere around the fake reading of the will," he admitted.

Did she realize how much she cradled her stomach?

Rory battled against the strong urge to protect her. He'd only push her away. Cadence's independent streak had always been longer than the Rio Grande. She might be stubborn but she wasn't stupid.

"You're right."

He almost performed a double take. Was she agreeing with him? Did she have another agenda that she was about to lay down?

"I know you want to go back to Colorado. Promise you won't make that decision without at least letting me know before you leave?" he asked.

She blew out a breath. "Believe it or not, I'm not trying to make any of this harder than it already is, Rory."

Somehow, he doubted that. But he didn't want to send her blood pressure up again, so he didn't comment. "Does that mean you'll discuss your plans with me before you act?"

She cocked an eyebrow. She looked good standing there in the kitchen. Even better than he remembered and that was saying a lot. Was it the pregnancy making her skin glow? He'd heard horrible things about what pregnancy did to a woman's body and yet it sure as hell looked good on Cadence.

His fool heart squeezed at the thought of her having his child. First, he had to get them both out of danger.

"You have a right to know where I am."

He bit back the argument that said he'd had a right to know about the baby from day one but she hadn't exactly shared that information until she was forced to. In fact, if he hadn't shown up, he would still be in the dark. But all he cared about right now was finding the guy who'd called himself Dex.

"Dalton asked about anyone you can think of who might be upset with you," he continued. "Have you thought of anyone? This guy said his name was Dex but he'd be an idiot to use his real name and he didn't strike me as naive." The whole camping scene had been set up to look like Dex was a less-experienced outdoorsman. The guy was better than Rory had initially given him credit for because he'd slipped out of Rory's reach.

"Seems like having Butler for a last name is enough to put me on the wrong side of a rifle scope," she said with a frown. "But no one comes to mind."

"Fair enough," he said, feeling her frustration peel off her in waves. "Until we figure it out, you'll need to keep a low profile."

"Understood." She pinned him with her stare. "What's going to happen to Boots?"

He gave a noncommittal shrug.

"Dex was obviously using him as a decoy, so there won't be anybody looking for him. I'd like to keep him here at the ranch if you don't want him," she said, and he couldn't figure what she'd want with the little dog.

Rory had only briefly considered keeping the puppy for himself. Taking the dog on the range while tracking poachers wasn't the best-case scenario for the dog or Rory. A wrongly timed bark could put Rory in grave danger. He'd be no good to the dog dead. Rory's life was smoother if he traveled alone.

Plus, a home with Cadence would offer far more stability than anything Rory could propose. This was the first thing they'd agreed on since the baby bomb had been dropped just hours ago. Rory still hadn't wrapped his mind around being a father. Figuring out the rest that came along with it was going to be a slow climb. As far as the dog went, he could give her that. "Okay."

What was up with the empty feeling that

overcame him at the thought of giving up Boots? It wasn't like he had enough time to train a dog or the lifestyle to support one. Sure, Boots was cute but Rory couldn't have truly bonded with the animal in such a short time. A voice reminded him that he'd always wanted a dog and that was most likely the reason for the melancholy that wrapped around him at the thought of giving up Boots.

He looked at Cadence, who was staring him down, and he could tell that she was trying to figure out what he was thinking.

Ella broke the moment when she entered the kitchen. She froze as though she realized she might've been walking in on something.

His talk with Cadence was progress and Rory would take any ground he could gain with her. Another pang of guilt took a swipe at him for leaving her to deal with the pregnancy on her own this long. If he'd stuck around, he would've known.

"I had to wake a few people up, but everything's been set up for—" she glanced at the wall clock "—noon today."

Rory glanced at the same clock. That didn't give him much time. He locked on to Cadence's gaze, trying not to think about the way her silky skin goose bumped when he skimmed his lips across that spot on her hip, the one on her right side. Or the sexy mewl she made when he slid his tongue over her stomach and then across her bare breasts. *Good job, Scott. Way to be strong.* He cleared the frog in his throat before meeting Cadence's gaze again. Her face was flush, which almost made him wonder if she was thinking about the same things. No. Definitely not. She was probably just having a hot flash, or whatever pregnant women had when they wanted to strangle the man standing across the kitchen island from them. "I know I said you'd better rest but now I'm thinking you should pack a few things instead."

"You're right." Again, he was caught off guard when she didn't argue. "I'll be back in a few minutes."

Rory turned to Ella. "You might want to get a few hours of sleep, too, before everything goes down."

"I doubt if I could," she said. "I'm not feeling well from all this stress and I don't want to wake up Holden."

He'd heard about her husband. Holden seemed like a good guy. Rory could see himself going fishing or having a beer with him. Of course, now that news about his and Cadence's so-called quiet fling was out, no Butler or Crawford would ever trust him again.

Ella moved to the fridge and pulled out a ginger ale.

"Congratulations, by the way," he said. "I hear you and Holden got married over Thanksgiving."

She smiled. "Holden's leaving for Virginia tomorrow. He has a few things to take care of back home."

"I was hoping to meet him and shake his hand." It seemed like everyone was coupling, finding happiness.

"He'd like that," Ella said.

Rory figured family life was in the cards for some.

Not him.

His collar tightened just thinking about settling down. He tugged at it but it didn't loosen. He glanced around, wondering if someone had turned the heat up.

"You okay, Rory?" Ella asked. She walked over to him and zeroed in.

No. He felt like he was going to pass out. But he wasn't about to admit to her the idea of becoming a father made the air whoosh out of his lungs and the room shrink. Or maybe it was just the thought of marriage doing that to him.

"Fine."

"Tell me what you need and I'll get it for you," Rory offered, and it immediately occurred to Cadence why he would say that. The feeling of being hit by a bus slammed into her. The rifle had been trained on *her* window. There was a shooter out there who wanted to put a bullet in *her*. The depth of those statements was starting to sink in. She wasn't as concerned about herself as she would've been six months ago, which seemed strange. Times had changed. She had other lives depending on her. The thought that anything could happen to her babies almost knocked her back a step.

Anger shot through her and she could only imagine how much stronger her protective instincts would become once the twins were born and she held them in her arms. For a half second she thought about telling him there were two babies. Deep down, she feared it would be too much for him. That he would get spooked and take off again.

Rory would be protective of them, too.

Would he fight her for custody? She'd been

immature before. Made big-time mistakes. Would Rory use them against her in court?

"Cadence." Rory snapped a finger near her ear.

"What?"

"I asked about your things. What should I pack for you?" he asked with a concerned look.

"Oh. Right." She shook her head as if that could get rid of the bad feeling. "I'll go with you."

He seemed reluctant to agree.

"I'll stand at the door far away from the window," she said.

His lips compressed into a thin line, which was a sign of anger for most people but it meant she was making progress with Rory.

"All right," he finally said, turning on his heel.

It didn't take long to pack, considering Cadence hadn't completely unpacked yet. Still, she only wanted to take a change of clothes and a few bath products. Rory placed them in her old backpack from high school that was in her closet, saying it would be easier to carry them around this way. He added that it would also be easier to slip out unnoticed.

"So, what's the plan exactly?" she asked.

"Mr. Staples is coming through the front gate at around eleven forty-five. There'll be a slew of activity out there as his car arrives. Ella plans to be in the front, looking like she's finishing decorating. We'll slip out the back. There'll be a four-by-four waiting for us."

"Sounds easy enough," she admitted.

"But then we're going off road toward the east side of the property," he said. "Think you'll be okay going over a few bumps?"

She rubbed her belly. "I guess so."

"Don't worry. I'll take it as easy as I can," he said. "The four-by-four vehicle will get us to farm road 12 where a vehicle is parked."

"What about Dex? Think he found it?" she asked.

"We'll see when we get there." He zipped her pack and threw the strap over his shoulder. "Ready?"

She was so ready to get out of there. Being at the ranch without her father was hard. The events of this morning had distracted her but nothing felt the same without Maverick Mike Butler around.

Waiting for the right moment to slip out the back door seemed like it took an eternity. She'd eaten and thrown a few protein bars in her backpack to tide her over just in case. It seemed like she was always hungry these days since she was eating for three.

A small group of ranch hands went out every day on four-by-fours to check fences and keep an eye on the herd, so she and Rory joined the caravan that split in opposite directions once they cleared the barn.

Her nerves were frayed thinking that Dex or someone might be out there, waiting for them. An ambush could easily be set up even with all the precautions they were taking.

And then there was Rory. Being in close contact wasn't a good idea. Her body seemed to remember all the nights they'd spent together and ignored her brain that was telling it to cool its jets. There was something about pregnancy hormones that made her crave sex even more once she'd gotten over the initial hump of wanting to vomit on everyone. Hormones were strange.

Wrapping her arms around Rory reminded her how easy it was to be with him and how built he was. Then there was the excitement of keeping their fling to themselves, telling no one about their relationship. It seemed so much purer that way without her family's interference.

Plus, she doubted her father would've

approved. He didn't like her seeing hired help socially.

Those endless nights with Rory came rushing back into her thoughts, showering her with memories. Memories of lying there tangled in the sheets, gasping for air, completely happy. Memories of staying up half the night talking. Memories of waking up in his arms the next morning.

Was it the happiest she'd ever been? Yes. She could admit that part to herself. She'd been happy with Rory, which had made his ultimate rejection sting all that much more.

SNEAKING OFF THE ranch as the family lawyer arrived had worked as planned.

"Where to now?" Cadence asked as Rory navigated onto the two-lane highway.

"I have a place on the outskirts of town." Rory's place had always been viewed as his personal haven so he never brought people there. Cadence Butler wasn't exactly "people," considering she was the mother of his child, an annoying voice reminded.

She got quiet and he could only guess his revelation had hit her in a bad place. This was her first visit.

The rest of the ride was spent in heavy silence, like a storm brewing.

The fact that he cared about Cadence's opinion of the small cabin tightened the coil that was already overly wound up in his gut. It was one of the reasons, okay the main reason, he'd insisted they meet up somewhere else when they were together.

She moved from the living room to the dining room, the kitchen and back. He couldn't read her expression. Was she disappointed?

"One bedroom?" she asked and for the first time in probably her life, she sounded nervous.

"All I need," he said a little too quickly. He glanced at her bump and decided the first thing on his to-do list once she was safe was find a bigger cabin or start plans to add a room to this one.

He studied her expression as she took in the place. Frustration nipped at him that he couldn't tell what she was thinking and he sure as hell didn't have any plans to ask. His small cabin wasn't big enough or good enough for someone used to living in a place that looked like some high-end resort. She had people who cooked for her. She'd most likely never cleaned up after herself a day in her life. To say his place was modest would be putting it lightly.

She quirked a smile before taking a seat on the leather sofa.

"What?" he bit out a little harsher than he'd intended. He was frustrated that her approval meant so much to him.

"Nothing." She shrugged, looking offended at his sharp response. "I just didn't expect you to have any furniture."

"That's fair." He smiled. He couldn't help it. "There are dishes, too."

"How about a pillow and a blanket?" She bit back a yawn and when he really looked at her, she had dark circles under her eyes.

"In the other room where I want you to sleep." He motioned toward the door off the living area.

"I'm fine right here. This couch is actually comfortable," she suggested.

"It'll work for me." He walked over to her and offered a hand up.

She didn't take it. Instead, she pushed up to standing and then walked past him.

Chapter Six

If Rory thought Cadence was incapable of finding a glass by herself he needed to think again.

Even so, she was surprised that his place was so cozy. A corner fireplace made of tumbled stone anchored the living room. A simple mantel consisted of a long darkly stained wood plank. Instead of the obligatory massive flat-screen TV every bachelor seemed to have, Rory had a wall of shelving with keepsakes and a few books.

The place felt so much like him. She didn't want to feel this comfortable at his place. She could also clearly see that his cabin was meant for one—a number Rory liked. She'd been sucked into believing he had real feelings for her once. And for Rory, he probably had. But he could only go so far before he cut himself off from emotions that could make him want to stick around. Now it was her turn to laugh. Rory Scott staying in one place for more than a few days? Now, that was funny.

"Let me know if you need anything," he said from the door.

"Okay." She peeled off her ballet flats, thinking how much water weight her ankles held now. Let her eat one potato chip and they'd swell.

It was nice to climb under the covers. Even though it was early afternoon by now, she was tired. Lack of sleep and pregnancy weren't friends. She immediately drifted off and felt like she'd barely closed her eyes when an urgent-sounding voice shocked her awake.

She tried to mentally shake off the fog and force her eyes open. It didn't work. She had the feeling that came with being in a deep sleep and something jerking her awake. It was like moving in slow motion. She forced her eyes open to confirm what she already knew. It was Rory. He was standing over her, gently shaking her with a serious expression on his face.

"Wake up, Cadence," he said again with more urgency this time. His voice was laced with anger, too.

"What's wrong?"

"Someone followed us." She heard him mutter a string of curse words before glancing at her and apologizing. "Someone's here."

"Where?" she asked, pushing up to a sitting position. And then she heard a noise outside. "Never mind. What do we need to do?"

He set her ballet flats on the bed next to her before locating a fold-up chair from the closet and positioning it against the closed bedroom door.

"Be as quiet as we can," he said in a whisper.

She rubbed blurry eyes in time to see that he was clutching a rifle with his left hand as he checked and then opened the window.

The urgency of the situation hit full force when Cadence heard the wood floor creak in the next room. Her pulse raced and her hands started shaking as she slipped into her flats.

Rory was beside her in the next instant, taking her hand and leading her to the now-open window.

Panic roared through her at what they might find outside. In broad daylight, it would be harder to hide.

Rory helped her out the window before following her in the next heartbeat. It was clear

by the stealth and quickness of his movements
that she'd wind up holding him back.

He broke into a run toward the thickest part
of the trees surrounding the cabin, which happened to be around back. She thought about
the angry lines etched in his forehead when
he'd spoken to her. Did he resent the fact that
she would slow him down?

"Can you run a little faster?" he asked as
she heard the back door of his cabin smack
against the wall.

"There," a strong male voice said and she
didn't dare risk a glance back. She was already having a hard time keeping up.

She struggled for purchase in the slick-bot-
tomed shoes she wore.

Another voice cut through the air and
ripped down her spine. The men had seen
them and were coming. She pushed harder,
ignoring the burn in her thighs.

Throwing everything she had into moving
faster, she caught the side of a large rock at
an odd angle and rolled her ankle. She tumbled and her first thought was the babies. She
prayed they'd be okay as Rory helped her up.

He looked like he had to make a quick decision, help her or keep the shotgun.

With no time to evaluate her injury, he

chucked the weapon and they took off running again, this time without her right shoe because there was also no time to hunt for it. Rory was the only thing keeping her upright.

Adrenaline couldn't completely mask the pain pulsing from her right foot as she felt every sharp rock and branch against the pad of her foot.

Whoever was behind them would gain ground if she so much as glanced down to see how bad it was. She could feel a cool liquid running down her ankle and it made her foot slick. She had no idea what she was stepping on…a mix of rocks, branches—creepy bugs?—or who knew what else. Cadence involuntarily shivered at the thought of crunching a cockroach with her bare foot.

A grunt escaped and she felt Rory's hand tighten around hers.

"I'm okay, keep going," she quietly urged, knowing full well he'd stop if he thought this was too much for her. She couldn't afford to be the reason they were caught and especially since someone wanted to put a bullet in her head.

In the thickest part of the trees, she couldn't see twenty feet ahead. She knew that Rory had done that on purpose and yet it slowed

them down, too, as they winded through underbrush and weaved through mesquite trees.
He started zigzagging and she was pretty sure
he'd circled back to where they'd started—it
all looked the same to her out there—when a
pair of men jumped them from behind a bush.

Instincts from having brothers who loved
to wrestle with her when she was growing
up caused Cadence to throw up her elbow instead of panic. She connected with the face
of a thin but wiry man. Wiry grimaced and
then threw his arms around her in a viselike
grip. She dropped down and twisted, breaking his hold on her.

Rory was nearby and he lunged at Wiry,
knocking him off balance. He looked at Cadence and shouted, "Run."

She hesitated for a second because she
didn't want to leave him alone. Plus, her ankle
was screaming with pain.

Rory was strong. There was no doubt about
his fighting ability. But two against one?

Rory made eyes at her as he pinned Wiry
down between his thighs.

She pushed to her feet, almost lost it and fell
when a branch jabbed her heel, but powered
through enough to run.

A football-player-looking man dove at Rory.

He twisted out of the guy's way but he was in for a fight. If she weren't pregnant, she would've stayed to help but she had to put the babies first and that's what Rory wanted.

The voices behind her grew faint until they disappeared. Cadence pushed as hard as she could, considering her right foot felt like it had been shredded.

By the time she located a water source, a creek, she was barely able to make progress on that foot. Pain screamed at her and she was hobbling, grabbing on to anything that would keep her upright.

Cadence plopped onto the earth beside the rushing water. She eased her foot into the stream before flipping off her left shoe and doing the same with it. The cool water soothed her aching feet and gave some relief to her swollen ankle. Both of her feet were filthy and in pain but all she could think about was Rory and keeping her babies safe. She wished she knew what had happened back there after she'd taken off.

Another thought struck. She was alone in unfamiliar territory. She had no idea how to get out of the woods and Rory might not be able to find her.

The creek pooled ten feet downstream and

she glanced at the surface for water moccasins. Also called cottonmouths, these snakes were venomous and aggressive, and they seemed to be in every creek or lake in the state of Texas.

She glanced around, scanning the area, aware of being vulnerable to an animal attack unless Wiry and/or Athlete found her first. Was there anything she could use to stand and maybe help her walk? Better yet, was there anything around that she could use as a weapon?

Sticks? Branches?

Those things had done serious damage to her foot already. In fact, she'd have to figure out something because walking with her ankle swollen might not get her very far. Then again, sticking around could put her and her babies in worse danger. Cadence wiped away a tear that sprang at the thought that her babies weren't even born yet and she was already having trouble protecting them. Would she be a good mother? Could she be a good mother when she'd had no examples of one from her own parents?

She might not live long enough to find out.

As she swept her hand over the ground, she made contact with a sizable branch. She pulled it over to her, aware that her muscles were already screaming at her from all the movement and running.

Seemingly out of nowhere, a male figure appeared from behind her. She gasped and spun around to get a better look.

"Rory." Tears sprang to her eyes.

"We have to go," he urged, as he moved next to her and helped her to her feet.

Cadence dug deep to stand and his gaze flew to her bad ankle.

"Did you lose your shoes?" She remembered him being intense before but not so angry. What had happened?

"One is all I have left." She motioned toward the left shoe.

He immediately slipped off his tennis shoes and offered them to her, muttering a curse.

"These are too big." About three sizes in her estimation.

The sound of branches crunching caused her to gasp again. And then there were voices.

"We've got to go." Rory glanced around, and there was a desperate quality to his features that she'd never seen before. *Her fault?*

Feeling responsible for someone else when he had always been such a loner seemed to create a whole new hell for him and his emotions were playing out on his features so clearly.

He slipped her left shoe on before standing and taking her arm to pull it over his shoulder.

"Lean on me." He put an arm around her hip and she ignored the fission of heat that pulsed through her at the contact. This wasn't the time to think about how well their bodies fit together or how intense and satisfying their sex had been. "Will you be okay?"

"Yes. Let's go." It wasn't okay, because angry pulses shot up her leg with every movement, but what was the alternative? Stick around and be killed?

Leaning on Rory, she was able to deal with the pain. She ignored all the electricity vibrating from where they touched, chalking it up to her body remembering how incredible they'd been together in bed. Sizzle and passion may have made for the best sex of her life—and created the two biggest gifts—but it didn't make two people compatible outside the bedroom. And when she really faced the situation honestly, most of life happened in the other rooms. What good was the hottest sex if it didn't translate into an amazing relationship?

The fact that he'd been able to sneak up on her without making a sound earlier made her realize just how good he was at his job—a job that was as necessary as breathing to Rory.

She didn't know how long they'd been running but everything hurt and there was no sign of the men who'd been chasing them.

"Can we stop?" she finally asked, gasping for air.

"Not yet," he responded with no such sounds of struggle. She'd always known Rory was in tip-top shape; remembering the ripples in his muscled chest wasn't helping matters in the attraction department. But he wasn't making any noise breathing. No panting. No gulping air. *Seriously?*

After what felt like an eternity, he finally slowed the pace before stopping. He put his other hand up to make sure she knew to be quiet. She was doing the best job she could under the circumstances, because she hadn't run like that since high school track and she'd been a sprinter, not a pregnant woman who had fallen off her strict exercise routine a couple of years ago. She'd worked the ranch and that had made her strong, but it wasn't the same kind of cardio she needed for this.

Rory crouched low and listened. There was so much intensity to his actions.

She did the same but couldn't hear much over the sound of her own breathing.

Glancing at her feet, pain registered. Her right ankle looked like Shrek's. Her foot had been jabbed by sharp tree limbs and looked angry. She wiped at the blood to reveal fresh cuts oozing more of the red liquid. She had no idea where she and Rory were and no idea how to get out of the woods.

Pain throbbed from her ankle to her hip as adrenaline faltered and she started to shake.

And there was Rory, looking at her like she'd just punched him in the face.

What was his deal?

Rory cursed under his breath. What good did it do him to have skills if he couldn't keep Cadence and her baby safe?

He dropped down and examined her ankle and then her foot, ignoring the frissons of heat that came with touching her. This wasn't the time to think about those long silky legs wrapped around him as he drove himself home.

A mental headshake loosened the inappropriate image. He missed more than great sex with Cadence. She was intelligent, fiery and had a sense of humor that had calmed him down even when he was wound tight after a tracking job. To be honest, that had happened more than he cared to admit. A voice reminded him that it was easy for her to be carefree. She had her father's fortune to back her up and hadn't suffered a day in her life. Deep down, he knew that wasn't completely true or fair but he wasn't in the mood to argue with himself.

Getting her and his child to safety was priority number one. *His child. Damn.* That was going to take some getting used to.

"You can lean on me the rest of the way," he offered.

"Okay." She winced as she stood and a fire bolt shot straight through him. None of this should be happening and now he was damn certain the rifle being pointed at her bedroom window was no coincidence. He thought about having to ditch his own shotgun because he hadn't accounted for enough variables. Hell, it was his fault that she was in this position to begin with. His mistakes were racking up.

Leaning her weight against him sent a lot of other feelings he couldn't afford swirling through his body. He gripped her waist a little tighter, noticing how much fuller her hips had gotten because of the pregnancy. It was sexy on her, he thought, even though he shouldn't have allowed himself to notice.

He glanced down at her right foot, noticing the amount of blood. He did the best he could by making a field bandage with his undershirt. Cursing himself again for not having supplies out here might not be productive, but he did it anyway.

At least she didn't have to walk on the foot. She could lean on him for support and hop on her left. He'd made a critical error in underestimating the enemy. Rory hadn't seen anyone follow them to his place but those two guys must've done just that. It was the only explanation for why they'd shown. But who was after Cadence and why? There were more questions looping through his thoughts. None he had answers to.

After walking for a half hour, she doubled over and took in a sharp breath.

"What happened?" Panic tore through him like a tornado strike.

"Cramp," she said and there was desperation in her voice.

"Has this happened before?" he asked.

She nodded as he supported her weight.

"What do you need me to do?" Rory had never felt so helpless in his life.

Another sharp breath and this time he had to ease her to her knees. She grabbed her stomach as her face turned red. "Do you have cell reception out here?"

He palmed his phone and checked the screen for bars. "No. There's no cell tower out here to pick up a signal on."

Watching her bent over, wincing in pain because of his mistakes, shredded everything inside him.

"I need to get to the ER," she said.

No bars on his cell. She couldn't move with those cramps. Her foot was torn up.

An owl hooted and Rory tried not to put too much stock into the omen. Many local Native American tribes believed it to be a sign of death.

Anger ripped through him. No one was dying on his watch. He also knew that determination to live was often the dividing line between life and death in a survival situation. He knew Cadence. She would put up one hell of a fight. That spark was part of the reason he had fallen for her. The operative words being *had fallen.* When it came to emotion, he could only get so far before his warning system flared and he pulled back. Of course, his job made sticking around long enough to have a real relationship next to impossible. His feelings for Cadence had caught him off guard five months ago, causing him to retreat. It was most likely familiarity—he had known her since childhood—that had had him falling down the slippery slope of love. Love? Had he loved her?

No. He couldn't have. Rory didn't do that particular emotion.

The owl hooted again, bringing his focus back to Cadence. With her in this state, they'd be traveling even slower than they already were.

"How'd you get away from them?" she asked. "You were outnumbered."

"I know this area better. It gave me an advantage." The guys who'd caught up to them a little while ago were most likely still in the woods searching. It could only be a matter of time before the pair showed up again. These guys were new to the picture.

"Was it the guy from the campsite?"

"Nope." Neither one was Dex and that really threw Rory for a loop. He didn't have time to examine the implications right now, but he'd need to get this new evidence over to the sheriff as soon as possible. Any new information or lead could break this case and possibly Mr. Butler's murder open for Sawmill.

Rory had learned a long time ago that it was best to work with law enforcement rather than against it.

"Hold on," he said to Cadence, easing her to a sitting position.

He scouted the area and located the best tree to climb. Height could give him an idea of what was around and also if the pair of men on their tails were catching up.

Rory didn't doubt his tracking skills but a pregnant woman was not something he'd had to factor in before.

This was one in a long list of signs that reminded him he was in no way prepared for fatherhood.

But he was surprised at how deeply the thought of losing this baby cut into him and the bottomless well of anger that sprang up when he made mistakes that put Cadence and her—*their*—child in jeopardy.

Chapter Seven

"The coast is clear for now," Rory said through gritted teeth. He climbed down from the tree and helped her up. "A few more steps and we'll be near a clearing."

Cadence knew that he was frustrated with the situation and not at her. Although, she wouldn't have blamed him if he were considering how much she was slowing them down.

She was worried about the breath-stealing cramps, about her cut-up foot catching some kind of jungle disease—never mind that she wasn't actually in the jungle—and about never finding their way out of these cursed woods.

Thankfully, Rory seemed to know exactly where they were at every turn and she could see why he excelled at his job.

While she believed they were walking in circles—everything looked the same!—he cut a steady course toward freedom. Her injuries were slowing them down, though. She prayed the men stalking them were lost and far away because if they caught up, there could be more trouble than Rory could handle. In her condition, she was no help whatsoever.

"I don't want to leave you alone but I can hide you in a small cave not too far off the road and go get my vehicle. It'll give you a break from walking and speed up getting you to the hospital."

Just the thought of being tucked into a cave in her state was enough to cause icy fingers to grip her. What would be in there? Spiders? Snakes?

An involuntary shiver rocked her body. Her mouth went dry thinking about it. Then there was poison ivy. She'd learned a long time ago how allergic she was to it and remembered her childhood saying: *leaves of three, let 'em be.*

But what choice did she have?

The cramps were almost nonstop and there'd been no break in the pain pulsing up from that ankle. The worst part was that she couldn't feel the babies move and that scared her more than anything else. She'd had cramps before and her doctor had reassured her that everything was normal. But these felt different. More intense. Or maybe it was just the situation causing them to feel that way.

Cadence was tired, thirsty and she wanted to go home, take a warm bath and go to bed. A good night of sleep always did wonders to help erase a bad day. But this was more than that. Her life was on the line. Her babies' lives were threatened. And no amount of sleep could stop the people stalking her or erase this nightmare.

Since curling up in a ball and throwing her own version of a temper tantrum wasn't an option, she decided to suck it up and not complain.

"There won't be any creepy crawlies in there, right?" she asked, trying to sound as brave as she could under the circumstances.

"Shouldn't be. I'll double check if it makes you feel better." His steady voice was surprisingly reassuring and kept her nerves at a notch below panic.

"I can't believe I lost my shoe. Sorry to be such a hopeless case in an emergency," she said.

"You're not. You can't help what happened back there and you kept yourself and the child safe. Sometimes things get lost in the shuffle. You should be proud of the way you handled the situation," he said, and there was a hint of admiration in his voice. Or was that something she wanted to hear but didn't exist?

A wave of guilt hit her at not telling him earlier that she was carrying twins. This was definitely not the right time to distract him with the news. It had come as a complete shock to her and she could only imagine what hearing it would do to him.

Rory squeezed into an opening at the base of a small hill that looked like a lump of leaves. The trees in this area were thick enough to make it impossible to see in a straight line. There was a lot of underbrush to cover the opening, which most likely had been created by coyotes. Wolves? Or some other den animal. Okay, Cadence could admit that she was letting her imagination run a little wild.

Nothing inside her wanted to crawl inside the unknown.

Growing up on a ranch had taught her everything she needed to know about scorpions and snakes. With twin brothers, she'd had her fair share of spiders being tossed at her. The boys had grown out of those antics early on, but she still remembered the times when they'd come running at her with some creature in hand. She got the willies just thinking about it and it felt like a hundred fire ants were creepy crawling across her skin, ready to attack at a moment's notice.

But she was determined to do whatever it took in order to protect her babies, even if that meant facing some of her worst fears. Getting from where she was to the den was another issue. Okay, she could do this. Maybe not walk the entire distance with these mind-bending cramps, but she could get to the next tree. It felt like all the blood rushed from her as she sucked in a burst of air and planted her right hand on the tree trunk next to her. She could take one step. She did, pausing after in order to breathe and regain her balance.

Rory emerged from the opening. "Nothing scary in there."

"Great." She took in the distance between them. She could make it to the small boulder two feet in front of her…take another step or two.

"What are you doing? Hold on there," Rory said but it was too late. She made it to her next goal.

"I can do this," she said. So much of her life in the past year had been about taking one step at a time, not looking too far ahead because her head might explode.

The next thing she knew, Rory was beside her. She took in a breath meant to fortify her before taking hold of his outstretched arm.

One more step. She could make it to the mesquite tree near the opening.

Getting inside the small opening was the easy part. Not letting her imagination run wild was going to take some effort.

"A few more steps and you're there," he said in that low timbre that was so reassuring.

She knew on some level that Rory wouldn't put her in jeopardy. At least not on purpose.

"I'll be back as fast as I can," he promised before his face disappeared. She'd known that he was good at his job before but seeing him in action brought her awareness to a whole new level. She didn't hear one single tree branch break or a hint of Rory's footsteps. He was like a ghost and it was even more apparent to her how much she must've been slowing him down and how much attention she had been drawing with her heavier footsteps. Her right foot felt every scrape, rock and branch.

Rather than focus on the amount of pain she was in, and it was staggering, she decided to recap what she already knew.

There were at least two men after her, three counting Dex.

Why?

Cadence searched her memory to find anything she'd done that could make someone want to take her life. But then, like she'd said before, being a Butler was dangerous and especially while her father's killer was still on the loose. Her siblings had had brushes with criminals and the law. Thankfully, they'd come out on top.

Other than her half sister, Madelyn, Cadence hadn't had a disagreement with anyone recently. Heck, she'd spent the past few months in Colorado, so she really drew a blank as to why she'd be targeted the second she came back to Cattle Barge. It made sense to focus on everyone she knew locally.

She heard footsteps outside the den and immediately knew that it couldn't be Rory. He'd been stealthy before.

Cadence listened.

"Any sign of her over there?" one of the male voices asked in a hushed voice.

"Nope." She recognized the voices as belonging to Wiry and Athlete.

A mind-numbing cramp hit and she bit her bottom lip to stop from screaming. Blowing out a breath was too risky. Fear seized her. What if Wiry and Athlete had gotten to Rory?

She heard the two men stomping around, making so much noise that animals and birds scattered.

Rory must've covered her tracks. Of course he would think of doing that and probably several other things a less experienced survivalist wouldn't. She'd never been more grateful for his skill set because that was most likely the only reason the men weren't walking right over to her and dragging her out of the small den. If hiding had been up to her, she would never have been so clever.

She just prayed she could keep quiet until they moved on.

"Hey, come over here and look at this," one of the men said. She thought it was Wiry but everything had happened so fast earlier she couldn't be certain.

Her heart clutched. Had they found her?

Oh, no. She felt around for a stick or something she could use as a weapon. Even though it was light outside, she couldn't see a thing. It was dark inside the little den and that made it a good hiding spot. Not so great for her nerves as she felt something crawl over her left wrist. *Please don't scream. Please don't scream.* The thought of anything happening to her babies clamped her mouth shut. There was no pain so great that she'd put her little girls in jeopardy.

Slowly, quietly, she focused on taking longer breaths. She breathed in through her nose and out through her mouth like she'd learned in yoga class last year in order to calm her racing pulse.

A few minutes passed and she realized the voices were gone. She listened a little longer, breathing as quietly as she could. More minutes ticked by and she had no idea how long she'd been in there or if it was starting to get dark outside. What time was it anyway? Ever since she'd started carrying a cell phone, she stopped wearing a watch. Not having her electronic devices set her nerves on edge.

Suddenly there was activity at the mouth of the den.

"It's me." There'd never been a better sound than Rory's voice.

Relief flooded her.

"They were here. They almost found me." She grabbed on to his hand and used it to shimmy out of the den. As soon as she was free, she threw her arms around his neck and leaned into him. His body felt so good and warm against hers after lying on the cold ground.

He muttered a curse low and the sound of his voice calmed her racing heart.

"It'll be dark soon. We should move," he finally said. "How are the cramps?"

"They aren't better and they aren't worse. There's hope in that, right?" The question was rhetorical and when she got a good look at his face, she could see how dark his features had become. Dark with frustration? Regret? Or worry? It was probably just wishful thinking, but she hoped for the latter.

She wanted to know that he cared and told herself it was reduced to primal survival. Offspring of most species had a better chance of survival if the father was involved in their care. But then she thought about lions and bears and how males would kill a cub. She'd seen that on a nature show once while she was nursing a sick stomach early on in the pregnancy.

Rory wasn't like that, her mind reasoned. He'd do whatever it took to protect his own. He'd already demonstrated that. It was her fool heart wishing that he'd done it out of his feelings for her. That he could love her and really be there for her.

She leaned her weight on him as he helped

her to the conversion vehicle on the side of the road.

Once inside, she finally felt like she could exhale.

"I have a few emergency supplies, water and ibuprofen," Rory offered.

"Water would be nice," she said.

He rounded the back of the vehicle, popped open the back door and then returned a minute later with a bottled water in hand.

She took the offering before he climbed into the driver's seat and pulled up the nearest hospital on his GPS.

"I hope we're far enough away that no one will recognize me," Cadence said. Getting away from a place had never felt so good as leaving those woods. Emotions filled her and released in the form of hot tears. She turned her face toward the passenger window, away from Rory and did her best to conceal the tears.

"That'll be tricky. Nurses and doctors have to maintain confidentiality, so even if they realize who you are, they won't be able to tell anyone," he said.

"True." She hoped her name wouldn't leak. "Hitting an out-of-the-way location should keep us out of the paparazzi nightmare. I think they have someone stationed at the hospital, the funeral parlor and every restaurant in the town."

"Since you've been out of town, there aren't a lot of recent pictures of you being posted and hardly anyone knows about the pregnancy," he said.

"Right again. If I see one more picture of me from my high school yearbook, I might scream."

"It's cute." Rory laughed and so did she. Another cramp cut the moment short, but levity felt good and she liked putting a smile on Rory's face.

Puppies were cute. She wanted to be a gorgeous woman in Rory's eyes. He'd made her feel every bit of that and more during their fling.

"First to the ER and then to the sheriff," he said.

"Agreed." Another thought dawned on her. "If the check-in nurse doesn't recognize me, I'd like to give a fake name."

"That's a good point. We can check you in as my cousin, Hailey, from Oklahoma," he said.

"You have a cousin?" She spoke before reason kicked in.

"Of course I have a cousin," he countered and there was a hint of defensiveness in his voice.

"I guess I knew that." She knew it was possible, but Rory had never spoken about his family.

"She's on my mom's side and it wasn't like she came to visit before I took off," he added. "I met her a couple of times when we saw my mom's family around the holidays."

"You never told me what happened with your family. Why did you leave them when you were so young?" she asked.

Rory's gaze intensified on the stretch of road in front of them and he clenched his jaw. "Isn't much to tell."

With that, he put his blinker on and changed lanes.

"Okay then. I'm Hailey from Oklahoma," she said, trying it on to see if it felt natural. Even though she'd known the man next to her for more than a decade, he'd never shared anything about his childhood or his parents with her. It struck her as odd after they'd been intimate that she knew so little about his background. She could tell by his change in posture that the subject was a sore one, so she didn't press. But was it possible to really know a person without knowing where they came from?

Another thought struck. "But what about insurance?"

"I can figure out a payment plan. I'll put the bill in my name and we'll tell the truth. We don't have insurance," he said.

"There's no need to do that." She had a sizable trust and would be inheriting one-sixth of the Butler fortune. There was no reason that Rory should have to struggle to make payments. She wiped away her tears and looked at him when he didn't respond.

Anger practically radiated off him. Was it about the money?

When she really thought about it, her brothers would want to pay if one of them were in this situation. Had she just insulted Rory by not wanting to put him in a financial bind?

"Hospital fees can be really expensive for the silliest things," she continued, and another look at Rory said she was digging a deeper hole.

Why was he so hard to talk to?

ONCE CADENCE WAS checked in to a hospital room and settled Rory needed to get some air. The fact that he had no medical insurance to cover a baby let alone her visit to the ER sat in his stomach as though he'd eaten nails. He'd worked and saved his money, so he had a small stash of cash. From everything he'd heard, babies were expensive and he wouldn't be able to take the risks he took now. The thought of how much his life was about to change almost paralyzed him.

He was in no way ready to bring a child into the world. He'd forgotten to ask Cadence about the due date with everything else going on but it couldn't be too far off. Wasn't pregnancy nine months? She looked to be at least halfway there. Maybe more. Although, he was the last person to be able to calculate a due date.

And how the hell had this happened?

Rory had always been careful. There'd always been a condom because he'd never wanted to be in this position.

Now that he was picking the situation apart, he realized that it wasn't even the unplanned pregnancy that had him twitchy. It was Cadence. She'd been hiding this news from him for months. Sure, he'd ended the fling but didn't she trust him at all?

Granted, he'd been on the range in Wyoming, where he didn't exactly get cell coverage most of the time, but Cadence was resourceful. If she'd wanted to reach him, she could've.

That annoying voice in the back of his head piped up again, reminding him how clear he'd been about wanting space from her. The high truth was that he'd needed her to move on before he did something stupid, like ask her to marry him and force her into a life well below what she was accustomed to. A life that would make her miserable.

The stubborn look in her eyes when she'd told him to go ahead and leave that day five months ago had faltered. Hell, his parents had spent a lifetime making each other miserable in the name of love.

As strange as it might sound, Rory cared too much about Cadence to ever let it come down to that.

Rory wondered if his folks were still together. He hadn't spoken to either of them since taking off at fifteen after one of their world-class brawls. His mother had broken the lamp over his father's forehead, swinging it like a baseball bat after he knocked her into the wall. Drywall had broken her momentum, which had been so intense the wall had given. Picture frames had flown off. The glass in them had shattered long ago. His mother hadn't bothered to replace it. Even she knew it was only a matter of time before the next all-out fight with her husband.

The worst part wasn't witnessing the fight. That was bad, don't get him wrong. Horrible. And he tensed up thinking about the abuse. But his mother making excuses for her husband after made Rory sick to his stomach. She'd roll up her sleeve to reveal several bruises and tell him that's how she knew his father loved her. She'd said a man wouldn't fight with a woman he didn't have passion for.

Rory had known at a young age how twisted that logic was. He'd tried to convince her, too. But she'd smile at him and tell him that he had a lot to learn about relationships. If that was love, Rory wanted no part.

His sister, Renee, who was two years older than him, had kept him sane during all the screaming matches. When she'd taken off at seventeen years old to follow her musician boyfriend across the country, Rory had seen no reason to stick around at home.

A job on the Butler ranch and a room in the bunkhouse had saved his life and kept him out of serious trouble. Mr. Butler had covered the legal arrangements. Rory's friendship with Dade and Dalton had been a lifeline during his teenage years. And how had he repaid the family? By having a secret fling with Cadence, getting her pregnant and then walking away. Granted, he hadn't known about the pregnancy but he wasn't ready to let himself off the hook.

Way to go, Scott.

Sarcasm couldn't make a dent in his frustration with himself. He clenched and released his fists a few times, allowing a blast of frigid air to strike as he walked into the parking lot.

There was no question that he'd do the right thing by his child. Part of that was going to be getting along with the baby's mother.

Rory made a couple of rounds in the parking lot to burn off his excess energy and focus. Exercise always had a way of clearing the clutter in his mind and helping him find his center.

By the fourth lap, he realized that if he and Cadence were going to get along, the first thing they'd have to do was establish trust.

The fact that she didn't trust him was his fault. He could own that. Because he'd walked out on her and she probably assumed he'd do it again. On the drive over, she'd asked about his background and family. He'd gone quiet on her. The odd thing was that he wanted to tell her. Maybe it was to release some of the frustration and shame that he couldn't fix his home life.

Either way, she needed to know that he planned to be in his child's life and that meant being part of her life.

Damn, it wasn't like he didn't have feelings for her. He could use those to develop a friendship, right? Anything more was too risky with his blueprint for relationships. There was no doubt in his mind that he would never put a hand on a woman. That was without question. Hurting someone in the name of love—as his mother had always tried to make him believe—made even less sense to him.

But every time he tried to talk to Cadence, he ended up frustrating her and the last thing he wanted to do was argue. They'd made a little progress in his vehicle when she'd cracked a joke. But that had barely made a dent in the distance between them.

As it was, she stood on one side of the river and he stood on the opposite. There had to be a way to build a bridge so they could meet somewhere in the middle and especially for the child's sake. He could admit that being near her brought up old feelings—feelings he'd shoved down so deep that he hadn't thought they existed anymore. Dwelling on them was as productive as putting a Band-Aid over a bullet hole.

Speaking of which, his finances had been on the right track. He'd been taking some risks in order to amass more money. Stupidly, he thought he could find a magic sum in his bank account that would allow him to take care of Cadence in the right way. Taking care of the ER visit might put a healthy dent in his savings account but he'd do whatever was necessary to step up as a father.

A few deep breaths followed by repeating his favorite mantra—*patience, silence, purpose*—to psych himself up and put him in the right state of mind to check on Cadence.

Rory walked back inside the hospital and located her room. He stopped when he heard voices inside. There was a male voice that he recognized as the doctor's from earlier. He didn't feel right intruding, so he stood outside the door and listened, hoping to hear good news. The look on Cadence's face when she was cramping earlier had him worried that something might be wrong with the pregnancy. He couldn't even think about something going wrong with her health.

"I know you said you were worried about the lack of movement in the past few hours but both babies look good…"

Both? Did that mean what he thought? *Twins?*

Anger roared through him at the thought that he'd been deceived twice.

First, she'd hidden the pregnancy and then she'd lied to him?

Rory didn't realize he'd started pacing until a concerned-looking nurse stared at him. He cut right and took a few steps down a different hallway so he'd be out of the line of sight of the nurses' station.

Several trips up and down the stairs got his blood pumping and helped stem some of his frustration. Besides, Cadence was already in enough distress. He didn't want to make the situation worse.

He located Cadence's floor and pushed the door open, ramming the metal edge right into a janitor's back.

"Sorry about that," Rory said.

The guy didn't turn and look at Rory. He waved a hand and then took off in the opposite direction in a hurry.

There was something about the interaction that caused Rory's warning bells to sound off.

Cadence.

Chapter Eight

Cadence's door was closed and that sent another warning flare soaring high into the sky. The fact that he'd left her alone when he should've stayed put and kept vigil over her punched him. His temper had put her in danger.

Rory muttered a few choice words as he beat feet, wasting no time in getting to her room. His instincts were finely tuned because of his work on the range and those predispositions were screaming at him to get to Cadence.

He blasted through the door in time to see a nurse inserting something into Cadence's IV.

"Stop," he commanded severely. "Step away from her and drop that thing in your hand."

A flash of fear followed by determination darkened the medium height, medium built, brown-haired nurse. "I'm sorry, sir. But you can't be in here."

"Like hell I can't." He darted to the nurse as she tried to sidestep him. He shot a glance at Cadence. "Get that thing out of you."

She sat up with a panicked look on her face as she jerked the IV out of the vein on her right arm.

Rory tackled the nurse and the two of them flew into the side chair.

"Call for help," he shouted to Cadence.

"I hit the panic button as soon as I got a look at your face," she said, and he registered the sound of an alarm coming from the nurses' station. "What should I do?"

He was on top of the brown-haired nurse, pinning her arms to her sides with his thighs. "Can you get dressed?"

"Yes." She immediately moved to get her clothes, walking tenderly on her bad ankle. He saw that she had on some kind of compression boot that was giving her structure and support and he was glad for that at least.

But damn. He'd put her in jeopardy again. She was injured and needed him to be solid for her and all he could think about before was his anger. It was the curse of his parents to put himself first over others in his life and let anger override rational thought.

"Who are you?" he asked Brown-haired.

Before she could respond, a blond-haired nurse popped her head inside the door. "What do you need, sweetie—"

Panic rippled across her features as her gaze swept the room.

"Annalise, are you okay?" The stress in her voice was meant for the nurse on the floor.

"Your friend here just tried to drug my friend," he bit out.

"Help," Annalise said, and he almost wished he had knocked her out so she couldn't talk.

The door closed, the nurse disappeared and Cadence looked at him with a helpless expression. It was only a matter of time before security showed.

"What do we do now?" Cadence asked.

He'd tell her to run but there was no use. She couldn't get far and Brown-haired would most likely scream. She already was, in fact.

He reared his fist back and looked her dead in the eyes. "Keep it up and I won't hesitate to shut you up myself." The threat was idle but she didn't know that.

Based on the fact that she clamped her mouth shut, she believed him. And that was a relief because nothing inside him could ever allow him to strike a woman.

"What did you put in her IV?" he barked.

Tears sprang from Annalise's eyes. Her lips compressed into a thin line and she shook her head.

Footsteps fired off in the hallway. He was running out of time.

"Annalise, you have one chance to get this right. Tell me why you did this and I won't press charges." She'd have hell to pay for her actions as soon as Administration figured out what she'd put in the IV. "At the very least, you're looking at losing your job and a lawsuit. At the worst, jail."

Annalise's brown eyes widened.

"I'm dressed," Cadence said. "Let's get out of here before everyone comes back."

"We're safe. It's this one who should be worried." He held Annalise's gaze. "That's right. They'll lock you up and throw away the key, Annalise." He could see that he was gaining ground with her. "And I'll testify to exactly what I saw. The evidence supports my story, by the way."

She faltered, her chin quivered, and it looked like it was taking great strength to keep her emotions in check. There was so much fear in her eyes and something else, too. Helplessness?

"I'm sorry." Her gaze bounced from Cadence and Rory. "What have I done?"

"Nothing, because I stopped you," Rory ground out.

"I'm a single mom and he said he'd kill my kids if I didn't put that in her IV." Her desperation caused her chin to quiver again as tears streamed down her cheeks. "It's no excuse but I was so scared."

"Did he say what the substance is?" Rory shouldn't have been shocked when tears streamed down her face but she'd caught him off guard. Her tortured expression punched him.

"No and I didn't ask. How was I supposed to make a choice?" Annalise shook her head. The thought of having to choose between a pregnant stranger in her care and her children twisted her face with guilt. "I didn't want to know."

He could relate to her conflict because he had a similar one going on inside. Hurt a single mother's career when it sounded like she was the only parent to a pair of kids or throw justice to the wind. She wouldn't have done this if not for extreme circumstances.

The door burst open and a man wearing a security uniform barreled into the room. He was middle-aged, his hair a solid white, and Rory could take the man down in a heartbeat if he wanted. Instead, he put his hands in the air. "We don't want any trouble."

"This is a huge misunderstanding, Robert," Annalise said with a glance toward Rory. "I'm okay."

Rory hopped to his feet and held out a hand. She took it in a show of trust. "We don't have a problem here."

"I made a mistake, which caused a problem. None of this is their fault," Annalise admitted as she sat up. She was trying to force even breaths. "I'm one hundred percent to blame for this. I take full responsibility."

Cadence stood in between the security guard and Rory as she mouthed, "It's time to go."

"Hold on, ma'am. That's not advisable." The nurse who'd been standing behind Robert took a step beside him.

"I'm leaving and there's nothing you can do to stop me, so save your energy." Cadence folded her arms and glared at the nurse standing next to the security guard.

As far as security went, Rory couldn't imagine what an overweight fiftysomething man could accomplish. He'd be no match for Rory. But he had no intention of getting into a fight or pushing to see how far the guy would take that stun gun resting in his palm. Robert had come in hot, geared up for a fight. And like a cornered animal, he'd come out fighting.

"It's fine, Meredith," Annalise soothed. "Like I said, totally my fault. I tripped on his shoe and we both fell over. This guy was checking to make sure I was okay before he let me get up. That's all. I'm sorry I yelled earlier. It's under control." Annalise said it like it was nothing, like she was brushing lint off her scrubs.

Based on her scowl, Meredith wasn't buying the excuse. She wore her skepticism like a billboard, front and center with a spotlight trained on it. One eyebrow cocked, she asked, "Are you sure you're okay, Annalise?" She made eyes at her coworker.

"Yes." Annalise wiped her hands down her scrubs again. "I'm a little shaken up from taking a tumble. I knocked my head on the tray stand and took a pretty good fall. But

I'm good." She lifted her arms up and made a show of giving herself a once-over. "See."

"Where do we sign out?" Rory asked Annalise.

"I'm afraid I can't advise you to do that," Meredith interrupted.

"Either way, we're walking out that door," Cadence insisted.

Meredith stood there for a minute, staring into Cadence's eyes. "Are you sure you want to risk your babies?"

Cadence's chin jutted out at the suggestion she'd do anything purposely to hurt her children. "You need to do a better job of keeping people safe in here. A stranger walked in and started tampering with my IV and where were you? I think my babies and me will be safer on our own."

It was Cadence's turn to shoot a furtive glance at Rory and he saw a flicker of emotion behind her eyes. Guilt?

She'd lied to him. Again. Building a bridge between shores seemed insurmountable but none of that mattered right now. He needed to get her out of the ER.

"She wouldn't hurt her children," he snapped at Meredith, who drew back as though he'd physically punched her.

The woman could think what she wanted. Cadence might be a handful and she wasn't being honest with Rory, and he was presently upset about that fact. But no one could say she wouldn't be a good mother.

He moved to her side and urged her to lean her weight on him before walking her out the door and to the elevator.

Once inside, he pushed the *L* for lobby.

"Thank you for what you said back there about me being a good mother," she said once the doors closed and they were alone again. "Did you mean it or was it your way of telling them to back off?"

"Both." He took her hand and stormed out of the hospital. He led her to the passenger side of his vehicle and then took the driver's seat. He gripped the steering wheel and bit back his anger. "When did you plan on telling me there was more than one baby?"

"LATER. WHEN I THOUGHT you could handle it." Cadence should've come clean with Rory from the beginning. There was no good answer for her actions, so she leaned back against the headrest and pinched the bridge of her nose in an attempt to stem the raging headache forming between her eyes. The cold had ripped right through her while walking to the vehicle and the frigid air caused her brain to hurt. At least she had a compression boot on her right ankle now and that was giving her relief. She'd refused pain medication, even though the doctor had reassured her she could take a low dose.

"What the hell is that supposed to mean?" Rory's voice was low and steady, angry.

"I still can't figure out how I'm going to take care of one baby, let alone two," she admitted. "I'm sorry I didn't tell you but—"

"No excuses, Cadence. If we're not honest with each other there's no point in trying to candy coat this. The babies will suffer and I don't want that." He was right.

Cadence took a minute to let those words sink in. "We're not off to the best start, are we?"

"No, but it doesn't have to be that way." Again, Rory made sense.

"I can do better. I want to do better. The babies deserve it." Maybe she and Rory could establish some common ground from which they could build some trust. She shelved her fears that he'd ultimately take off, leaving her to hold the bag for the time being.

"What about the sex of the babies?" He paused a beat. "Do you know?"

"We're having daughters," she supplied.

"When?" His voice gave away nothing of his thoughts. But that was Rory. He needed time to digest.

"I'm due in March but my doctor warned me they could come early." An odd feeling of relief washed over her at spilling the details. She'd kept the news about the girls to herself so long. Talking about them, about the pregnancy made it feel less daunting.

"That's soon," he said and she could tell the news was sinking in.

It didn't feel all that soon for her. But then she'd had more time to reconcile the pregnancy.

"Girls," he said low and almost under his breath. There was a reverence in his tone that warmed her.

"That's right."

"Have you thought about names?" he asked and then held up a hand. "We can discuss the babies later. Right now, we need to find a place to hide out for a few days."

His statement closed the subject for now. She could almost hear the questions swirling in his thoughts, questions he must have.

Talking to him about their daughters felt better than she knew to allow.

"I'd like to make contact with Ella or one of the twins to make sure everything is okay on the ranch," she responded.

"We can do that before we stop off to rest." Rory pulled off the highway. He bought one of those pre-paid phones that didn't require any identification or a credit card. "No one can track this phone back to us."

Did she want to know why he was so adept at hiding in the shadows? Or why that life was so appealing to him? What did that say about him? Did this have anything to do with his upbringing? All she knew for sure was that he sure seemed comfortable with all this. Whereas she was so far out of her element it wasn't funny. At least the nurse was able to put some magic salve on her foot to soothe the cuts and insect bites.

Rory handed the phone to her once they were back inside his truck.

She called Ella's number. The line rang but her sister didn't pick up. "She won't answer because she doesn't recognize the number."

"Too many reporters calling?" he asked.

"Yes, among other unscrupulous people." The call rolled into voice mail so she left a message. "I know she'll listen to it, so we should wait a few minutes to give her a chance to call us back."

"While we wait, can I ask you a question?" His tone was deep, serious, and that sent a warning ripple through her body.

She sat straight up.

"You can ask me anything, Rory."

Chapter Nine

"Why didn't you contact me when you found out you were pregnant?" Cadence couldn't read Rory's emotions based on his steady tone but her heart dropped anyway. Should she admit just how brokenhearted she'd been when he walked out and slammed the door behind him? How devastated she'd been when days turned into weeks and weeks turned into months without hearing from him?

What good would it do to admit it to him now? An annoying voice in the back of her mind reminded her that nothing would change between them no matter how many heat-of-the-moment revelations there were.

She'd had a crush on him from the day she'd seen him in the barn on that cold October morning when he'd come to live and work on the ranch. They'd grown up around each other but not together. She'd spent the first summer doing the most ridiculous things trying to get him to notice her. Fifteen seemed so grown up compared to a twelve-year-old. She'd picked up a cigarette butt and had pretended to be smoking to seem older to him. And when he'd told her those things will make you sick, she'd dropped it faster than a hot iron skillet handle.

When she'd embarrassed herself in the barn trying to kiss him, she'd given up. He hadn't noticed her much anyway except for being kind to her like the other ranch hands were. She'd lost interest when he'd given her no sign of sharing her affection.

She'd gone away to college and he'd started tracking poachers. He rarely ever came back to Hereford but the few times he did when she was home on break caused her stomach to flip. Old times, she'd told herself. Unrequited love and all that.

And then late last spring had happened—a wild fling with the best sex of her life—and he'd regretted it so fast that he'd broken up with her, walked away and never looked back. He was only in Cattle Barge and on the ranch because of a job, because of work offered by her brothers.

"By the time I found out I was pregnant I had no idea where you'd gone," she admitted. That part was true. Could she have found him? Probably. Her brothers didn't seem to have trouble locating him in order to offer a job.

He shot her a look that said he was thinking the same thing she was.

"Be honest. If I'd asked you to come back without telling you the real reason, would you have?" she asked.

He stared out the front windshield for a long moment.

"Guess we'll never know."

He didn't speak it out loud but he was right. Being forced back together wasn't the same thing as coming together voluntarily. The pregnancy clouded everything. Plus, he'd shown up at the ranch for a job. When it came to their relationship, he'd walked out once. And since history was the best predictor of the future, he'd do it again. If she weren't in danger, would he have stuck around this long? She doubted it.

But then she didn't figure Rory would desert his own children.

The throwaway cell phone buzzed and that could only mean one thing. Ella's call was perfectly timed to break the awkward tension filling the cab.

"Are you okay?" Ella's voice was frantic.

"Yes. Had a close call," she admitted, owning up to one of them. "But Rory is here and we're safe for now."

"Where are you?" Ella asked and then immediately said, "Never mind. Don't answer that. I'm just happy that you're not hurt. I've been worried sick about you and the baby."

Rory grunted.

She ignored him. This didn't feel like the right time to share the news she was having twins.

Cadence understood why her sister would be in a panicked mode. Each of the Butlers had been targeted or involved with someone who'd been targeted for murder since their father's death over the summer and the bad news didn't stop there. They'd found out about dozens of lawsuits trying to lay claim to their land and their father's fortune. It seemed the whole world had spun out of control following their father's death and Cadence felt like she hadn't gotten a chance to mourn his loss. Colorado had been more of an escape. Being pregnant and so very sick that first trimester had distracted her. Or maybe she just couldn't face the fact that her father was gone and never coming back.

"I'm fine and the babies are good." Because of Rory, but she didn't explicitly say that. Ella would know. "What about at the ranch? What's going on there?"

"Not a thing. It's been quiet and that's why I was worried about you. That, and you haven't answered any of my calls or texts," Ella admitted.

"I lost my purse a while ago. Phone was inside. So no one bought the will being read early?" Cadence asked, remembering that Christmas Eve was Near. Wow, the first Christmas without their father. How sad was that? His presence would be missed so much. And her babies? She rubbed her belly. They would never know their grandfather. A tear escaped and she swallowed a sob. The sudden burst of emotions caught her completely off guard, but she was beginning to realize that pregnancy hormones had a way of bringing on the internal drama.

"Nope," Ella admitted.

"I don't like that," Rory said under his breath but loud enough for Cadence to hear.

She nodded because she was thinking the same thing. It meant someone on the ranch could be involved. There was no way anyone from security would allow themselves to be compromised or turn against the family, at least she hoped. Although, that could explain a lot.

"What about Ed? I thought he was out of town. Is that true?"

"Ed's in Amarillo. He headed there right after he left the ranch this afternoon," Ella supplied.

"If someone's tracking his movements, he should be warned," Rory said.

Ella gasped. "That's a good point. I'll call him to let him know as soon as we get off the phone."

A horn honked somewhere behind them, causing Cadence to jump. She glanced around, noting that someone was getting impatient for a car to relinquish its parking spot. Relief flooded her. Of course, the people trying to get to her wouldn't be making any noise to give her and Rory a heads-up that they were coming. Instead, there'd be a bullet flying toward her most likely aimed at her chest.

Again, Cadence couldn't think of one person who would want to hurt her or her babies.

"We better go," she said to her sister, needing to keep moving.

"Rory," Ella started. He acknowledged her. "Take care of my sister."

For once, it didn't sound like an insult. Cadence didn't mind having someone else watch her back and especially since the person was Rory. He might be angry with her and maybe even a little hurt—and she could give him that after hiding her pregnancy from him this long—but he would take a bullet for her if need be. She didn't question his loyalty to her and, even though he might not admit it yet, the babies.

After ending the call, a thought struck.

"Is there any way the person after me is trying to get to you?" she asked.

Rory's jaw fell slack for a split second, indicating that he hadn't thought of the possibility. He straightened in his seat and started the engine. "The guy with the rifle on your land had the business end pointed at your bedroom window."

"That still strikes me as odd when I think about it. How did anyone know that I was home?" she asked.

"The will reading was big news. There's no telling how long he'd been there. He could've been camped out on your property for days." Rory navigated onto the highway, put on his blinker and steered into traffic. "I know how to find out, but we need to find a place to camp for a few days to let your ankle heal."

"Christmas Eve is in four days. We don't have time," she said, noticing it was after midnight.

"I'm doing a lousy job of keeping you safe while running away from the problem," he said after a thoughtful pause. She ignored the double meaning. "I'm no good at it."

"Then where do you suggest we go?" Normally, she knew exactly where Rory would end up—out on the range where he could disappear without a trace. He was most comfortable there and he knew this area of Texas better than anyone. Even the Butlers knew less about their land, which was saying a lot considering the fact that they'd grown up on it and it was part of their souls. Of course, when she really thought about it, Rory had, too.

She remembered the day he'd shown up at the ranch as vividly as if it had happened yesterday. He wasn't a day more than fifteen years old. His hair was curly, a little too long, and his eyes a little too wild. He reminded her of the best of the land, untamed and beautiful in its own right.

Her heart squeezed a little more thinking about what her father had said about him...

That he reminded him so much of himself at that age. That he could be lost forever if someone didn't intervene and look out for the kid.

She didn't see any similarities between her father and Rory.

She'd had a crush on Rory from the minute he strolled—too casual a word for what he'd done, romped over her heart was more like it—into her life. Of course, she'd been his best friends' little sister. Three years age difference had meant a lot at twelve and fifteen. Now, it seemed like nothing.

"I have no idea," he said, but his voice lacked his usual certainty.

"There was a guy who came into my room before the nurse. I think he was a janitor," she said.

"How well did you see his face?" he asked.

"Not well. He kept his chin to his chest and he was wearing a ball cap." She pinched the bridge of her nose, trying to force a picture. "I didn't think much of it before because he blended in but after what happened with the nurse, the timing of his visit strikes me as odd."

"It does me, too," Rory admitted. "What else do you remember about him?"

"He was shorter than you and my brothers,"

she remembered. "I'd say he was five feet ten inches if I had to guess. He had on jogging pants underneath a gray shirt. But he looked like every other guy. I mean, he was pushing a mop and he took the trash can out."

"I saw him. He's the reason I rushed into your room," Rory said.

"Do you think it was Dex?" Cadence's voice cracked with tension.

"It's possible."

"How could he know about the nurse's kids?" she asked.

"That's easy enough to figure out at her area at the nurses' station," Rory said. "She most likely had pictures up and he figured he could use them to get to her. Whoever this guy is, he thinks on his feet."

"These are the kinds of people you deal with on a regular basis, aren't they?" Cadence asked, realizing how much he knew how to think like them. Would that be enough to keep her and the babies safe?

AFTER DRIVING FOR two hours straight, Rory pulled off the road at a familiar campsite. It was remote and hardly anyone knew about it, which was just the way he liked it. When he'd first walked out of Cadence's life, this is where he'd come to get a grip on his emotions so he could move on.

"Stay in the cab. I'll set us up," he said to Cadence.

"Are we camping in this cold? The radio said it was going to dip below freezing tonight," she said with a look of horror.

Rory suppressed a laugh. "No, I'm not going to let you freeze. Believe it or not, I'm damn good at my job and I wouldn't be if I got frostbite and lost my fingers or toes." He wiggled his fingers and smiled. The break in tension was needed to regain perspective. More often than not, perspective came with patience and silence.

He could admit that living on the range had lost some of its appeal lately. Being alone with no one to talk to after being with Cadence and not being able to stop thinking about her had made him soft. Doing his job meant keeping a sharp mind and everyone at a safe distance.

Cadence had made that difficult. Being with her made him think he had to make a choice between living on the range that he loved or being with her.

He climbed out of the cab and took in a deep breath. Being out of town and away from all the cars and activity, he could finally breathe again. It didn't help as much as he would've liked.

A world without Cadence had lost its appeal.

He was too young for a midlife crisis but feeling a complete loss of identity was the best way to describe what it had felt like to leave Cadence. He'd figured getting back on the range in the job he loved would be enough to fill the void. It hadn't been and he'd been wrong on both counts.

The tent on the back of his conversion vehicle was set up and ready to go in less than ten minutes. He'd done it so many times he could set it up in his sleep. He'd built the platform for a foam mattress long ago. He'd even rigged an extra battery to his truck's heating system for those freezing nights when he was too far from civilization to get back and needed a few hours of shut-eye.

There was a stash of power bars and coffee. He had supplies to make a fire and the setup for a pot to boil water.

Early in life, being on the range had been his solace. The feel of a light summer breeze on his skin had brought a sense of peace he'd never known with people, until Cadence.

Had she rocked his world? *Hell, yeah.*

But watching his parents had taught him that love was toxic, too. His parents probably didn't fight from day one, either. There'd most likely been a honeymoon period in which they'd gotten along before having kids.

Speaking of which, Rory wondered where his sister had landed. Was she still on the road with what's-his-name? Was she trapped in a bad relationship? Marriage? The last thing she'd said before she left home was that she'd rather die than end up like their parents.

Rory couldn't agree more.

"That's quite a setup," Cadence said, and the sound of her voice caught him off guard.

He hopped out of the vehicle's bed to help her climb inside.

She took his hand and he ignored the electricity shooting up his arm and the heat pinging between them.

"It's warm in here," she said, rubbing her hands together.

"Afraid all I have is coffee to drink." Warm liquid would soothe her throat and he wanted to give her as much comfort as he could.

"I'd take hot water right now," she said.

"Then hold on." He could do that. He gathered a few supplies and hopped out of the truck bed.

Fifteen minutes later, he was handing her a cup of warm liquid.

"I'm impressed, Rory," she said, taking the offering. "It's easy to see why you're the best at what you do."

"Being alone has its disadvantages. It doesn't always make me the easiest person to get along with," he admitted. He'd need to learn to give-and-take to make co-parenting a possibility with Cadence.

"We do the best we can, right?" It was a peace offering he would take.

He needed a minute to mull over his thoughts about what had happened at the hospital. All that stress couldn't be good for the baby, correction, *babies*. Rory couldn't even go there right now about suddenly having two lives depending on him.

Cadence's physical description of the janitor matched Dex's.

An idea popped about how Rory could find out. Local poachers may have seen Dex and his cohorts. One of the poachers could possibly lead them to Dex's location. Rory needed to find a way to infiltrate a poaching site while bringing Cadence along. That wasn't going to be easy. She didn't exactly fit in out there with her manicured nails and ivory skin, and especially not while she was pregnant.

But nowhere was safe and especially not in the city. The person or persons targeting her wouldn't expect her to be out on the range and that's most likely why Dex had started there. Rory could circle back to the original campsite for clues as to who this guy really was. There was another consideration. Dex might be a gun-for-hire but his identity could help lead them to his boss. Sheriff Sawmill needed an update, too. It was too risky to take Cadence to his office.

"What's going on? What are you thinking?" Cadence asked, breaking into his thoughts.

"I have a crazy idea."

"It can't be worse than sleeping in the back of a conversion vehicle in the freezing cold," she joked. He'd missed that quick sense of humor. He'd missed her smile, too, but this wasn't the time to make a laundry list of all her good qualities.

"This is going to seem like The Four Seasons compared to what I'm about to recommend," he admitted.

"Oh, no. It *is* worse, isn't it?" she asked on a laugh.

"I can always take you back to the ranch," he suggested.

She shook her head and she was right. He was just throwing it out there to feel like he was giving her an out. There was no out. There was only catching the guy involved and forcing him to talk. Rory reminded himself that he'd been doing a terrible job of keeping her safe so far. She had the cuts, scrapes and swelling to prove it.

A fresh sprig of anger sprouted, welling up inside him at his failures.

"Hey. Remember that time I was in the barn when you first came to the ranch? I was cornered by a rat and completely freaking out," Cadence said before taking a sip of water.

"I think you asked me to go get your dad." He chuckled. "You were practically climbing the walls."

"Do you remember what you told me?" she asked.

He thought about it for a while. "Knowing me, it was probably something stupid like stay put until I take care of it."

She practically pinned him with her stare. It was the one she had that said she could see right through him and wasn't buying anything he said.

"You told me that I was wearing your favorite color. Blue. Like the sky." She sounded a little offended that he didn't recall. "And that I should focus on that while you took care of things."

"And did you listen?"

"Yes. It kept me from panicking. I was able to calm down while you did whatever it was that you did to get rid of that thing," she said. "Ever since then I think of the color blue when I get scared. I think of the beautiful Texas sky and it calms me down."

Well, damn. How was he supposed to respond to that? "I was a know-it-all kid back then. I would've said anything to keep you quiet and hold on to my job. As I remember, you told your father about the rat and he gave me a pat on the back. Told me I'd done a good job."

If his off-hand comment surprised her, she didn't immediately show it.

The warmth on her face faded when she said, "Guess you'll say just about anything to get your way."

"Is that what you think?" Rory bit out through clenched teeth. He didn't like being called a liar and he especially didn't like the fact that all he could think about was kissing Cadence since he'd seen her.

There was so much heat between them that when she leaned forward he could almost taste her. She smelled like flowers and he figured she'd washed up while in the hospital.

Emotion overtook logic and Rory closed the gap between them until their lips pressed together. He couldn't ignore the pull she had, so he stopped fighting it.

He kissed her tenderly, afraid of doing anything that might hurt her.

She parted her lips and welcomed his tongue inside her mouth. She tasted sweet and exactly like he remembered—a fact that he'd thought about far too many times in recent months while alone on the range.

He brought his hand up to her neck and felt her pulse pounding at the base. The tempo matched his own as need stirred inside him.

On some level, he knew this was a mistake. It would only complicate matters between them and make him want things he shouldn't. But he couldn't care about that while she brought her hands up to tunnel her fingers into his hair and deepen the kiss.

Their breaths quickened as she scooted onto

his lap and repositioned until her full breasts were flush against his chest.

Rory dropped his hands to her sweet hips, which were fuller than before.

But that put the brakes on for him because it also reminded him that she was pregnant.

Running with his emotions instead of using his brain had gotten him into this mess in the first place—the one where his mind was convinced that he couldn't live without her and that scared him more than any physical threat he'd faced.

Plus, she was so damn sexy. He was already stiff and his length pulsed against her, so that made pulling back more difficult than climbing a rock covered in honey.

"Cadence." His mouth moved against her lips when he spoke.

She pressed her forehead to his. "Yes."

"Is this a good idea?"

"Probably not."

Silence sat between them, thick with sexual tension. It felt a little too good to be right where he was, to be holding her.

Cadence finally blew out a slow breath, the kind meant to garner strength. And then she climbed off his lap.

Cold air blew through the tent the minute

she pulled away. Or was it just his imagination playing tricks on him? Either way, he retied the straps of the small cloth window meant to let light inside and tossed on another layer before exiting the tent.

He'd almost let his emotions run wild and now all he could think about was that kiss. Just how much he'd missed Cadence was a punch to the gut.

Maybe they'd both be better off if he made other arrangements for her. Being this close was messing with his mind.

Was being this close to her a good idea?

If it only involved him, he'd say *no* and move on with his life. But there were other lives to consider now.

Could he be this close to Cadence and not fall for her again?

Not kiss her again?

Chapter Ten

Seventy-two hours of rest in a tight space had Cadence ready to climb the walls. Three more days passing also meant that Christmas Eve was tomorrow. Thinking about her father not being there for the holiday caused a physical ache. Everything was going to be different this year.

Her entire life had changed in less than half a year.

She placed her hand on her belly. Technically, next year would be her babies' first Christmas but ever since she'd felt one of the little bugs kick in her stomach, they were real to her. Before that, she'd felt like she had the flu for a few months and the reality of the pregnancy hadn't been able to sink in while she spent most of her time trying to keep food down.

"Good morning," Rory said as he slipped

inside the canopy. She hadn't heard him leave, or return for that matter. But when she'd opened her eyes a few minutes ago she knew he was gone because his side of the mattress was empty.

Cadence stretched sore arms and legs. The swelling in her ankle had gone down, which felt like a miracle.

"What time is it?" She felt lost without her cell phone or any of her usual comforts from home.

"Half past ten," he said, handing her a cup of warm water. "Wish I had something to put inside to give it flavor. Didn't you used to drink chamomile with lemon?"

"Sometimes." She was surprised he'd noticed those little things about her.

"This is better than nothing."

"What's it like out there?" She'd only left the pop-up tent to use the bathroom and take short walks. But she was amazed at how well Rory knew how to take care of injuries. He was used to relying on himself, on not having an ER on every street corner and she admired his independence. She always had and that was most likely part of the draw she felt toward him. That, and his ridiculous good looks. He had that rugged cowboy image nailed and his kiss had practically imprinted on her lips. She'd thought about it more than she wanted to admit in the last forty-eight hours.

"Cold." He smiled. It was the sexy out-of-the-corner-of-his-mouth smile and her heart free-fell.

Then again, maybe she'd spent too much time in a confined space. She was losing it.

"What's the plan? My ankle is better today and so is my foot," she said. He'd stopped off and bought a few supplies to make life more comfortable, one of which was hiking boots for her.

"Sticking around in one place too long is how poachers end up caught. So they're always on the move."

"That's poachers. We're looking for a murderer," she said.

"This guy used the same tactics I would've. I underestimated him before and that nearly cost us everything." There was so much self-recrimination in his voice.

"But we're okay. We're alive and I'm already healing nicely." Was he as hard on everyone else as he was on himself?

"My mistakes nearly killed you." Anger boiled up and she was close enough to see his steel eyes darken. He fisted his coffee mug and his knuckles were white.

There was no getting him to see reason when he was in this dark of a mood, so she didn't try. Instead, she grabbed the small bag of bathroom supplies he'd made for her and headed out of the pop-up camper.

This shouldn't have come as a surprise to her. She knew Rory better than he probably knew himself. Not long after he'd come to work at the ranch, he'd accidentally given cold water to a few of the horses after exercising them and that had made them sick.

He couldn't have been there longer than six months when it happened and Carl Hambone—or Bony Carl as everyone like to call him—had covered for him before chewing him out royally. Cadence remembered stopping at the barn door when she'd heard shouting. Bony Carl was an old hand and it took a lot to rile him.

She'd already had a crush on the young new hire, so she couldn't help but listen to what Bony Carl had said to her father. She'd been shocked that he'd taken full responsibility. Said he'd gotten distracted with a sick calve and then took the fall, saying he gave the horses cold water after exercise. They'd come close to losing two due to colic.

Rory must've heard, too, even though she didn't catch him listening at the time. The very next morning, he was up early and had packed his stuff. He didn't own much more than the clothes on his back. His entire life's worth of items barely filled his rugged, worn denim-style backpack.

She'd stormed into his room in the bunkhouse and had demanded he tell her exactly what he thought he was doing.

Rory had told her that he had to go. That he'd done something wrong and it was time to move on. He'd told her to leave it at that.

She'd planted her balled fists on her hips and dared him to try to get past her as she blocked the door.

"You'll listen to reason and that means owning up to your mistakes, Rory Scott," she'd said as she blocked the door.

"Is that right?" he'd asked.

"Yes. There's no use running from your mistakes. You have to face them or they'll just follow you and grow bigger than you can imagine," she said all full of sass and spice.

"That's what you think I'm doing? Running away?" he'd asked.

"That's what it looks like to me," she shot back, thinking she'd just nailed it.

"I told your father what I did," he'd said.

"And then what happened?" She was tapping her foot like an angry schoolteacher staring down an out-of-control class.

"I got fired."

Her jaw fell slack and she couldn't hide her mortification. "There's no way. I'll tell him he can't do that—"

"Your father has every right to take care of every animal on his property. He can run the place as he sees fit." Rory threw his backpack over his shoulder and stalked straight toward her. "Are we done here?"

And because she'd somehow convinced herself that he actually wanted to kiss as much as she did him, she threw her arms around his neck, closed her eyes and leaned forward to plant a big one square on his lips.

She could not have misread the situation any more.

Embarrassment flamed her cheeks just thinking about it. He'd turned his head to the side in time for her to miss. And then he'd gently taken her wrists and peeled them off him.

"Are you trying to get me shot?" he'd asked incredulously.

"No," she'd defended.

"You're twelve, Cadence," he'd said with that same self-recrimination she'd heard a few minutes ago in his voice. "I'm a teenager. It's not right for me to kiss a sixth grader."

She didn't figure this was the time to point out to him that he hadn't. And she'd known even then that he was being gracious by saying so.

Years later, when they shared a proper kiss, she'd pointed out that she'd been waiting a long time to kiss him.

"That's a lot of pressure," he'd said. And then he kissed her until her heart pounded her ribs and she had a difficult time catching her breath.

By then she was a grown woman and he a virile man. And the age difference from twenty-seven years old to thirty didn't seem like such a wide gap anymore.

She flushed thinking about how hot the sex had been.

The past three nights she'd slept with him, bodies pressed against each other for warmth.

Sleep had been fitful, worrying about what might happen, or if Dex, Wiry and Athlete, or someone else, stumbled upon their make-shift campground.

And then there was her heart. She'd moved on from Rory.

So why did her thoughts keep circling back to that kiss?

RORY DISASSEMBLED THE pop-up tent in less than ten minutes.

After hanging around the camp for a few hours, it was time to go. Especially after waking for the second time with Cadence's soft body against his, remembering how incredible the feel of her silky skin was as she lay next to him.

Besides, his thoughts kept wandering back to the kiss they'd shared the first day they'd arrived at the campsite. He performed a mental headshake to clear the image of her pink heart-shaped lips. The memory of how they felt moving against his wasn't helping.

Suddenly, the cold shoulder she'd been giving him seemed like it was for the best.

This was business, not personal. It was his job to keep her safe while the sheriff tracked down the person or persons hunting her. After three nights at this location, she hadn't come any closer to figuring out who could want to harm her. He'd cut them off from the world and her disappearance would be news.

One day until the will was going to be read.

"I know where we can go," Cadence said, returning with her bag filled with water, a toothbrush, soap and a washcloth.

"Where's that?" he asked.

"The barn."

Dozens of memories involving her and her family's barn tried to crash his thoughts. The bunkhouse had been the first place she'd made herself known to him. The thought of kissing a twelve-year-old when he was fifteen had felt all kinds of wrong, no matter how cute Cadence had been. Annoying, but cute. At fifteen, he'd felt like he was more of a man than a boy and she seemed so much like a kid in her highlighter-green halter dress and matching sandals.

He stared at her, trying to look deep.

"Think about it. It's perfect. Where's the last place anyone would expect me to go right now?" She wore the expression that said she knew she was right. Fist on right hip. Bottom lip in a slight pucker. It was damn sexy.

"Nowhere seems safe to me, but especially not the barn," he admitted. Again, a fist of guilt punched him. "That's my fault, Cadence."

"That's one way to look at it," she said. "As far as I can tell, you're the only one who's been keeping me and the babies alive so far. On our own—" she paused "—I don't even want to think about what would've happened."

Her gaze dropped to the ground and it looked like she was trying to hold back tears.

"I don't know if I expressed it before but I'm truly sorry about your father. He was a good man."

Cadence rolled her eyes and made a grunting noise. "I think we both know that's not necessarily true. I mean, don't get me wrong, he was my father and I loved him but he was no saint."

"He wasn't perfect. There's a difference. Most of his big mistakes were made when he was young," he said.

"Like having multiple children close in age? You know what that means, right? He wasn't faithful to my mother, and I've always wondered if that was the reason she took off or if she just knew she could never love us. And let's not forget the fact that someone hated him enough to want him dead." He moved close enough to see tears welling in her eyes. She turned her face away to hide them.

"It's okay to be emotional, Cadence. You don't always have to put up a strong front."

"Is that what you think I'm doing?" she shot back, her voice full of that spice he loved. Missed. The band around his heart tightened.

She was gearing up for a fight based on her disposition. Fists down at her sides were clenched so hard her knuckles were white. Her normally full pink lips compressed into a thin line.

He closed the distance between them and stood there. "Your mother leaving had nothing to do with you."

"If that's true, why does it still hurt so much?" She blinked up at him. He never realized the impact her mother deserting her could've had on her, the effect being abandoned would have on her self-esteem. He'd always seen the Butlers, and especially the girls, as being confident and privileged. He knew them well enough to realize their lives weren't perfect but he'd totally underestimated just how broken they could be deep down inside.

Rory recognized the emotion in Cadence because it was the same one he'd felt his entire life. That he was broken and no one noticed. The world around him kept on spinning. His parents kept on hurting each other and by extension him and his sister.

"I know how it feels." His words were meant to offer comfort, reassure. He was surprised by a sob escaping before she buried her face in his chest.

"What kind of parents can we possibly be to these babies, Rory? Neither one of us had a role model worth looking up to in the parenting department, and we don't even get along anymore."

"We can learn a lot from our parents' mistakes." This wasn't the time to debate their parents' failures. "They don't define us."

"I hid the truth from you. I know you, Rory. You'll never trust me again," she said. "How are we supposed to be good parents when we can't trust each other?"

She didn't say that he'd run away from her when their relationship had heated up. She didn't have to. He was already saying it to himself. And he was more convinced than ever that it had been the right move. Sure, it had hurt. He had the internal scars to prove that it had almost brought him to his knees. And yes, a weak part of him had wanted to show up on her doorstep more than a dozen times in the past five months. That was part of the reason he'd kept tabs on her whereabouts. His sensible side always kicked in and kept him from making a stupid mistake like that. He'd done that once when he let his feelings grow too strong for Cadence.

He would only hurt her.

Holding her in his arms, feeling her shaking, he knew that she deserved better.

Cadence deserved commitment, a white-picket fence, hell, a minivan if she wanted one. She needed a man who would walk through the door every evening without fail. With his job, and it was the only life he knew, he couldn't guarantee that.

When he really thought about it, the babies deserved more than that, too.

The thought of another man with Cadence and his children shot an angry fire bolt swirling straight down his spine. He had no right to feel that way if the two of them had no plans to get married and to bring up these children together. The fire bolt didn't care about logic. It burned a scorching trail down his back.

"There are two things I know for sure," he began. "One. And this is probably the most important. You are going to make an amazing mother."

She looked up at him with those big eyes and his heart stuttered.

"Two. We'll figure out how to take care of those babies together. We'll make mistakes but they won't be the same ones as our folks. I can guarantee that much."

"How are we going to do that, Rory?" There was a straight-up challenge in her eyes.

He didn't say by keeping a safe distance from her or by not kissing her again.

Because that's exactly what he did, kissed her.

"You're not making this easy." He said the words low as his mouth moved against hers when he spoke.

But great sex wasn't going to help the situation.

And the sound of a twig crunching nearby sent his pulse racing.

Chapter Eleven

Rory took Cadence's hand in his, linking their fingers. She followed him to the conversion vehicle that was ready to go. Her heart raced and she worried about the babies. She'd been under enough stress recently, between losing her father and the pregnancy, and now someone wanted to kill her.

She placed her free hand protectively over her stomach. Whatever else was going on between her and Rory, she was glad he was the one helping her. Granted, he'd been shocked to learn he was going to be a father and he had every right to be upset. But he also cared as much as she did about protecting the little ones. She'd already seen the look in his eyes.

"Get in." He motioned toward the passenger side as he released his grip on her hand.

Within a few minutes, they were clear of the camp, and they spent the next several hours driving around killing time. Her heart still thumped wildly but this time it was because she was thinking about the few kisses they'd shared. She needed to get a firm handle on her feelings for Rory, which had the annoying habit of careening out of control without notice. Hitting the wall in a fiery crash was certain if she let herself slip onto that racetrack again.

Cadence liked to think she learned from her mistakes. She and Rory needed to get to a good place with each other and that would begin with letting him know how much she appreciated everything he was doing.

"You've had a lot thrown at you all at once," she began. Admitting she was wrong wasn't the difficult part. Finding the right words to truly express it was more complicated. "I don't think I've thanked you for what you're doing for me and the babies."

"There's no need," he said without so much as a pause to consider her words. But that was Rory. He did the right thing like it was just expected, like everyone would. She knew it was part of his Texas upbringing, his cowboy code. Rory was not most people. No man from her past dating life had held himself to the same incredibly high standard.

"I'd like to anyway. I'm sorry that I didn't reach out to you sooner to tell you about being pregnant," she continued, wanting to explain but not make excuses. "I was so sick the first trimester." She saw his brow shoot up and realized that he wouldn't have experience with pregnancy lingo. "The first three months," she clarified.

He nodded his understanding.

"To be completely honest, I was terrified when I found out. You were gone, and I'm not blaming you for taking off and abandoning me. I could've handled the whole situation better." She understood him better than he thought. He would die a slow death if he couldn't be out on the range. She'd known it from that first summer he came to live on the ranch. He was almost as wild as the quarter horse her father had bought when he went through a horse-racing phase. The stallion her father had bought had a similar fire in his eyes as Rory. It was the first thing she'd noticed about the new hire when he'd come to work and live on the ranch.

Rory checked the rearview and she realized he was watching to see if anyone had followed them. That his gaze shifted back and forth a few times reminded her of the danger they were in.

"What did Sawmill say after your father was murdered?" Rory changed the subject. She could tell by his demeanor that she'd made progress and it was time to give the topic a breather.

"Everyone, including Sawmill, speculated that he'd gotten involved with a married woman because of the way in which he died," she admitted. "Sawmill explained that he was looking at someone close to our father or to the family because the murder was personal. It occurred while he was in his own bed in his room in the barn."

"Landry didn't see anyone coming or going." He stated the obvious. He was thinking out loud, which was the way he liked to talk through an issue.

"No. But my father didn't like to bring women in the house around his children and he also didn't like security knowing his business. He was private about his personal affairs. The main house was for family. His place in the barn was for..." She made eyes at him. "You know. His *other* activities."

"Who else did he suspect early on? Did he say?" Rory pressed.

"He said that it could've been a jealous ex or his current girlfriend. I spoke to my sister about that, and we can't imagine that Ruth would've done something like that and there was no evidence to prove she did. Besides, my sister and I had the feeling that Dad was going to announce their engagement soon. He must've been killed before he could ask her because Ruth didn't know anything about it. She said he'd been acting different lately and he'd hinted that he'd be making a big announcement soon. Ella and I thought the same thing."

"I can't think of a bigger announcement or lifestyle change than an avowed bachelor getting married," he stated.

"You made your views on relationships pretty clear to me five months ago," she retorted, wishing she could take the words back the minute she heard them coming out of her mouth. There was no reeling them in now.

He held up a hand in surrender. "I was talking about your father."

It still stung and her pride wouldn't let her admit that she'd ever wanted more from him than a casual relationship. So she shrugged it off, trying to come off as noncommittal. "Let's just move on."

"Fine by me." His voice was deep and tight. She'd hit him in a sore spot.

"A few of us were speculating that he was going to take a step back from some of his day-to-day responsibilities," she admitted, softening her voice.

"I'm surprised there wouldn't be some kind of communication trail that would give away what he was thinking. Emails? Receipts for an engagement ring?" Rory's tight grip on the steering wheel relaxed a notch, which was good. No matter what else was going on with them personally, they needed to be able to work together. Now, for her and the twins' safety. Later, because the two of them would have to learn how to co-parent. Tension between them would affect their girls and Cadence didn't want that.

"The sheriff didn't uncover anything in his investigation. Honestly, I wasn't all that surprised, considering how secretive my father was. We didn't even know that we had two other siblings until he brought them to the ranch through Ed," she stated. "All this time, we've had a sister and a brother and didn't know it. Dad kept his secrets until he was ready to reveal them and he'd been keeping those my entire life."

"I'm guessing that Sawmill didn't find any-thing unusual in your father's business ac-counts," Rory stated.

"Nothing so far. He brought in a few ex-perts to examine Dad's accounts and then he sent them off to another agency for a favor. They're still trying to untangle his relation-ships but there's nothing obvious there." She was already shaking her head. "You know my dad, Rory. His business, like his life, was complicated and private."

"A MAN DOESN'T amass the kind of fortune your father did by keeping things simple or blabbering about his plans to anyone who would listen." Rory should know. He'd spent more time than he cared to admit in the past five months trying to figure out how to do the same. After being with Cadence, he'd real-ized how lonely his life had become. In order to be able to go out and do the only job he was good at, he'd been forced to walk away from her for his own protection. He knew he was doing her a favor. But hearing the heart-break in her voice when she talked about the breakup was a face punch.

"Ed's been checking into all the paternity claims that have come up since my father's death. And there have been quite a few." He noticed that she couldn't bring herself to say *murder* this time.

"Again, he must be drawing blanks or he would've arrested someone by now," he said.

"Sawmill has interviewed everyone on the ranch. He put the ranch hands through hell. Carl and Dale have been with us the longest so they took the news hard. Anthony and Rupert were hired by my dad in the last year but they were both sick about the news. No one had any ideas of what could've happened. Of course, half the community thinks they know who would want my father gone but no one seems able to agree on a name," she said. "Hence, the reason I balked when you said my father was a good man the other day. If he was, there wouldn't be so many possible suspects."

"On any given day, people will love or hate you. When it comes to your father, ask one of his ranch hands how they felt about him," he stated after a thoughtful pause.

"They're loyal to my father. They would never say anything bad about him," she argued.

"True. But why are they loyal? None of them are stupid."

"Because he gave them a job." Her forehead wrinkled like that should be obvious.

"Have you ever worked for anyone who was a jerk?" he asked.

"I've only ever learned how to run a ranch," she admitted, and her cheeks flushed with embarrassment. "But I had a few pieces-of-work-type professors in college."

"Tell me about one of them," he said.

She rolled her eyes. "My history professor was the worst. He would come to class and only want to talk about current events but all his tests were from the test bank from the book. There were never questions from class discussions. He'd tell us something was important but it wouldn't show up on the test. It was infuriating."

"How often did you complain about him while you were taking the class?" Rory glanced at her quickly before returning his focus to the road.

"Pretty much every day," she admitted. "So I see your point."

"Your father gave jobs to a lot of good men over the years and he treated them—*us*—better than any other owner we'd ever worked for," he admitted.

"I think Rupert comes from a tough background. He's young. I think Dad wanted to give him a chance to make something of himself," she said.

"He might've been tough but we always knew where we stood with him. And he gave a few of us opportunities that no one else would've."

"He fired you for making a mistake six months after you arrived," she pointed out.

"True. And it was him who showed up after you left the bunkhouse and admitted that he was the one who'd made a mistake. Said he appreciated my honesty and gave me a raise because of it," he stated.

"I thought he hired you back after I yelled at him that night." An emotion flickered behind her eyes. Was it admiration for her father's actions? He hoped so, because it would be wrong to look at the bad side of her father and ignore all the good. Okay, Rory bit back the irony of that statement when it came to his own family. As for his father or any other man who got physical with a woman, even if she started punching first or baited him into it, had no honor.

"Sorry to disappoint you or make you doubt your ability to throw a good temper tantrum at age twelve," he said with a chuckle. "It was your father who showed me how to be a man and own up to my mistakes. It sure as hell wasn't mine." The last part came out with so much disdain it caught him off guard.

"Tell me something about your family, Rory. Why did you run away?" She turned the tables on him.

"My parents fought all the time. We couldn't take it anymore—"

"Hold on a second. Who's *we*?"

"Me and my sister," he stated.

"You have a *sister*?" Shock echoed from her voice. "And you never told me?"

"Guess it never came up," he admitted.

"I thought I knew you, Rory. How could I if I didn't even know you had a sister?" Cadence turned toward the window and crossed her arms.

He released a heavy sigh. Talking about his family wasn't easy.

"She's two years older than me. Her name's Renee. It was just the two of us growing up with our folks. I already said they fought nonstop. Mostly verbal but it got physical at times." He paused, trying to deflect the feeling of knife stabs in his gut as he dredged up the past. "Renee and I tried to convince our mother to leave him."

"And?"

"She refused. Said their fights were how she knew he loved her." He took in a frustrated breath. "There wasn't much we could do, so after a rough dust up Renee took off with a guy in a band she'd been sneaking around with. I didn't last long without her there, so I was next to go."

"Since you never mentioned this before and your family had trouble, I'm guessing you and your sister lost contact," she said.

"Yep. I'm not much on technology and didn't have one of these at fifteen anyway." He held up his cell phone. "I still don't have a social media account."

"Easier to stay under the radar that way," she guessed, and he nodded.

"I'm more of a light-a-fire-under-the-canopy-of-a-clear-night guy anyway." He shrugged. "So, no, I haven't spoken to my sister."

"Why didn't you look her up once you got older?" Cadence asked. It was a damn good question.

"I could say the same for her."

"So it's because you're stubborn," she said.

"You could say that. Last time I checked the phone rings both ways," he countered.

"Do you miss her?" she asked.

"We were close once."

"I'll take that as a *yes*." Cadence nodded toward his phone. "You know, it's not hard to look someone up on the internet these days. I can show you how to do it."

"I think I can figure out how social media works. What would be the point?" He pocketed his phone. "She could do the same thing and hasn't."

"You're a little harder to find for one. You track people for a living, Rory. And part of your job is making it as difficult as possible to find you, and yet you're mad at your sister because you think she hasn't even tried. You don't even know for sure and you don't see the irony in any of that?" She was walking on dangerous turf. An annoying voice in the back of his mind reminded him that the truth often hurt.

"What would be the point of getting in contact?" he asked.

"Seriously? Did you just ask me that?" Her voice was incredulous.

"She walked out on me as much as she did them. We both put the past behind us." It was easier that way. "What good would it do to dredge up those painful memories?"

"My father could be tough to deal with and he was especially hard on the boys. I don't know what we would've done if we hadn't banded together. We'd probably all be crazy by now." She shot him a look. "Sorry. I'm not saying there's something wrong with you."

"Let's talk about something else. Like who might be trying to kill you." He needed to change the subject because this was hitting a little too close to home.

Cadence sat there for a long time without speaking. When she finally did, she said, "Rory, I'm sorry about your folks. That's not fair to you or your sister. We didn't grow up in a house full of fighting and I bet that was hard on you."

Rory pulled into a pay-cash-as-you-go-type motel. The rooms-available sign had a couple of bulbs knocked out. "You'll be okay in here for the night?"

"Of course. A warm shower sounds amazing right now." Cadence sat there in the passenger seat as the sun dipped below the horizon.

"I'll be right back." He could keep an eye on the vehicle from the pay window.

He walked up to the thick plastic window, which looked like he was buying tickets for the state fair. A guy who was probably in his late forties looked up from the small screen he'd been watching.

"What can I do for you?" he asked.

"Need a room for the night." Rory kept his chin tucked to his chest because he didn't want to give away his identity. Not that—he read the guy's name tag—Phil seemed to mind.

"That'll be seventy dollars." Phil pulled a key ring with a plastic tag and held it out in front of him.

Rory took money from his wallet. He always carried cash. Staying off the grid helped in his line of work. Tomorrow night they'd be back in Cattle Barge. Rory couldn't deny that there was a certain feeling of rightness in thinking about being with Cadence on the ranch again. It was most likely because Hereford was where they'd met when they were just kids.

At fifteen, Rory might've thought he was grown. Experience had taught him a lesson about how much he had to learn before he'd be considered a man.

He slipped the exact amount through the metal slit at the bottom of a drawer.

When he returned to the vehicle, silence

sat thickly between them. Rory didn't want to talk about his family with her, with anyone.

"Speaking of sisters, we should give yours a call," he said.

Chapter Twelve

Room number three had a metal door and a large window with royal blue curtains. There were two beds inside. One looked like it dipped in the middle and Cadence didn't want to think about how many bodies it would take to create such a dent. There was a desk, a lamp and an old TV.

"This place isn't much." Rory handed her the throwaway cell phone.

"It'll do." She was determined not to make a big deal. Besides, a shower was a shower. The thought of a warm shower went a long way toward making this place seem better.

Cadence punched in her sister's number. Ella picked up on the first ring as though she'd been waiting for the call.

"How are you?" There was so much worry in Ella's voice.

"We're good," Cadence responded, hating

that her sister and the rest of her family were going through this again. She knew what it was like to stand by helplessly when someone she loved was in danger and it was the worst feeling. "Rory's taking good care of us."

She didn't look up at him when she said it because her cheeks flamed. She shouldn't be embarrassed giving him a compliment. Trying to deflect her reaction she added, "It's easy to see why he's considered the best at what he does."

Ella sighed in relief. "I'm grateful to him."

"Tell me what's going on at the ranch." She put the call on speaker.

Besides, she needed to change the subject. Going down that slippery slope of feelings for Rory wouldn't do her a bit of good.

"Preparations are being made for tomorrow night's will reading. Terrell and his team are on high alert and we brought in reinforcements to secure the perimeter," Ella supplied.

"That's smart. We'll need all the extra help we can get to keep everyone safe," Cadence confirmed.

"Who did you hire?" Rory asked. This was his field of expertise and he would most likely know the players.

"The Janson Brothers," Ella supplied.

"Good. They know what they're doing," Rory said. "How about the sheriff?"

"He's sending reinforcements. We're planning to get plenty of eyes on the ranch over the next few days. We also sent all our employees home to celebrate the holidays with their families. No one is even allowed on the property aside from May, of course." Hereford was home to May and she'd been a mother figure to the Butler children. It only made sense that she would stay for the reading.

"How'd they react to that?" Cadence asked. Everyone had been on edge since their father's murder.

"They were surprised at first, as expected. And then they were concerned. There were a lot of questions and speculation. You know how close we all are," she continued. "Everyone's worried about our well-being and no one wanted to leave. Ed did a great job convincing them that we'd all be safer if the ranch was cleared out over the holiday."

Hereford was family to everyone who lived there. The ranch hands and Carl developed brother-like relationships. Many of them had worked on the ranch for years. It took time to develop bonds like they shared.

"Will extra security make it more difficult

for us to come home?" Cadence asked Rory. She couldn't imagine that they'd waltz through the front gate and announce their presence.

"We can postpone the reading if you can't make it back safely," Ella offered.

Cadence knew it would require skill.

"We'll be fine," Rory said and she could tell by the tone of his voice that he already had a plan.

Ella heard, too, because she said, "Let me know if that changes. Otherwise, we'll plan to see you both tomorrow night at eleven thirty."

"We'll be there," Rory stated.

"Thank you for taking care of my sister," Ella said to Rory.

Normally, a comment like that would've been fingernails on a chalkboard to Cadence. In this case, she appreciated how many people were looking out for her because it was plain to see her sister was coming from a place of love.

"I love you, sis," Cadence said. She didn't say those words nearly enough to the people she cared about.

"I love you, too," Ella responded.

Rory stepped back, away from the receiver as though he'd intruded on a private family moment. He tucked his chin to his chest and turned his face away. Was he thinking about his sister, Renee?

Cadence and Ella exchanged goodbyes before ending the call.

"Where are we headed next?" Cadence knew he had their next move mapped out and she figured they would need to be close to Cattle Barge if they were going to be at the will reading.

"To Hereford."

"Right now?" She knew with one look in his determined eyes that he was serious.

"Ella said employees have been sent home. Anyone watching will expect us to show tomorrow close to the time of the reading." He made a good point. "I know how to get in and out of that bunkhouse unseen. I spent ten years of my life there." His jaw was set and his folded arms told her all she needed to know.

"Okay. Let's go home," she said with a certainty she didn't feel.

THE BUNKHOUSE HAD a common living area and kitchen with four bedrooms. Each had locking doors. No one ever used the locks but they were there.

Rory knew the layout better than the back

of his hand. He'd spent many a night there in his formative years.

Hereford had saved his life and he owed the ranch and its owner a debt of gratitude that he couldn't make up in a lifetime. Where would he be if not for the ranch? Prison? Dead? And that's the reason he could set aside his personal feelings about Mr. Butler telling him that he wasn't good enough for his daughter. Hell, Rory already knew that. One look at Cadence told him all he needed to know about where he stood. He couldn't figure for the life of him why she'd taken a shine to him when she could've had any male in the area at the snap of a finger.

Rory could name a dozen guys who would have made her much happier if she'd given them a chance. Men with normal schedules who could guarantee they'd be home every night instead of leaving her waiting in some two-bit shack like the place he owned. And yet the thought of Cadence with another man sent pure fire shooting through him.

His eyes had long ago adjusted to the dark.

He picked up the spare key to the back door of the bunkhouse from underneath a boulder next to the back porch. Ranch hands might be able to account for every member of a herd but ask any one of them to keep track of a set of keys and that was a whole other story.

After unlocking the door, he led her inside. It was past midnight and pitch-black outside. "We can't turn on any lights."

Cadence had been quiet on the journey over and he figured she must be exhausted. He'd taken her on a trail he used to ride every morning. It was the best way onto the property near the bunkhouse.

"I know we were just sitting but my legs are tired," she'd said.

"An hour's a long time to be in one spot." He'd had to be certain there was no one in the area before he would take her the final quarter of a mile to the bunkhouse.

"A warm shower and decent night of sleep would be amazing right now," she said.

"My old bathroom is on an interior wall and there are no windows in that hallway. As long as you keep the lights off, you should be good." He didn't want to think about her naked body in the next room.

"Not a problem. I remember when this place was built. I used to play on the slab of concrete before the walls came up. I know every inch. Don't need light to see." She disappeared down the hall.

Rory dug around and found clothes for both of them.

"Found a clean sweatshirt and jogging pants for you. They'll be too big but you can tie the waist off," he said, placing them on the counter.

He made himself a cup of coffee while she finished showering and dressing. And then he popped into the shower for a quick rinse before joining her in the living room.

"I still can't believe there were so many spare toothbrushes," she said.

"May keeps the place well stocked. Leave it up to the guys who live here and it'd be a sad state," he admitted with a chuckle.

"Too bad she didn't keep women's clothes in here," she said with a laugh.

The oversize shirt hugged her curves—curves that were sexier than he knew better than to let himself dwell on.

"Are you thirsty?" He'd managed to get a decent meal of burgers and fries in her earlier but that was hours ago.

"A cold glass of water would be nice."

He fixed another cup of coffee for himself and brought her ice water.

"Are you tired?" he asked, joining her in the living room. There was another thing he didn't want to think about and that was the day she'd stood at that door, fisted hand on hip, demanding he stop running. She'd been so full of sass and confidence. And then she'd tried to kiss him, which had given him a good chuckle at fifteen. She'd been a kid then. But the few they'd shared since seeing each other again were so damn hot he started stirring every time he thought about them.

The heat in those kisses had a habit of popping into his thoughts when he needed to stay focused on keeping her alive.

Speaking of which, he couldn't help but think the family would most likely be targets during the will reading.

Rory had every intention of ensuring that Cadence made it through the next few days alive.

Once this was over, it was going to be difficult to walk away again. Leaving her the first time had almost done him in. But now, with the babies, it was going to hurt punch-in-the-gut-like pain. The coil around his heart tightened and he took a minute to catch his breath.

This seemed like a good time to remind himself that he had a job waiting for him in Wyoming. A life on the range that he loved.

"Rory..." Cadence said, and he picked up

on something reverberating low in her voice as she scooted over next to him on the couch.

"What is it?" he asked.

"I'm scared." Her chin jutted out in defiance and he knew it took a lot for her to admit that.

"Nothing's going to happen to you or those babies on my watch," he swore.

"I believe you," she said. He could hear it in her voice that she didn't but he decided not to challenge her on it.

Instead, he asked, "Then what is it?"

"Don't let us end up like your folks," she said.

"That won't happen to us." That was a promise he could keep.

"What makes you so sure?" she asked and quickly added, "I know you would never lay a hand on me. I'm talking about the arguments. Words can be as damaging as a fist and that hurts kids just as much as when they hear their parents fighting. You know?"

"I do." Experience had taught him that was true.

She leaned into him, resting her head on his shoulder. It was most likely his being caught up in the moment but he wanted to be able to show her that he meant his words and kept his promises.

So he didn't debate his next actions. He put his hand under her chin and lifted it until her eyes met his.

And then he dipped his head down and tenderly kissed her.

She parted her lips and deepened the kiss. He slid his tongue inside her mouth, tasting her sweetness, which only intensified his hunger.

Primal need had him rearranging her until she was facing him on his lap. She eagerly complied, and his body had an instant reaction. Damn, she was sexy.

Heat ricocheted between them as her hands tunneled in his hair and her breath became ragged.

He wrapped his hands around her hips as she settled on his groin. His erection strained the second he realized she wasn't wearing panties. He dug his fingers into those sweet hips as she teased him with her rocking movement.

"Cadence," he said through quick breaths. His pulse raced at a staccato beat, pounding at the base of his throat.

He brought his right hand up to wrap around her neck and grazed his thumb across the base, a matching rhythm to his thumped against the pad.

"Do you really want to talk right now, Rory?" She froze long enough to look into his eyes. Even in the dark, he could see that hers glittered with need.

When she put it like that, she had a point. "No."

"Good. Because I want you to make love to me right now, Rory Scott."

That was all the encouragement he needed to keep going.

Until he thought about the babies.

"I don't want to hurt you...*them*."

"I'm not a fragile doll, Rory. I won't break and they aren't much bigger than my fist. There's no way you can hurt them." She crossed her arms and gripped the hem of her oversize shirt, freeing her generous breasts. He issued a primal grunt as he took one in his hand and then the other. Her nipples beaded against his palms as her mouth found his again.

He rolled her nipples between his thumb and forefinger, causing her to moan.

She brought her hands to the waistline of his jeans, fumbling around for the snap. She lifted herself off him, giving enough room for him to remove them. His stiff length ached to be inside her.

Her jogging pants hit the floor next, and she stood there naked and beautiful and everything he wanted in a woman. Her body was perfection but there was so much more to their chemistry. She was the perfect mix of spunk, intelligence and kindness.

He barely had his T-shirt off before she'd straddled him. Not long after that, she was guiding him inside her, *home*. Her silky skin against his rough hands nearly did him in, so he distracted himself by thinking about something else—anything else—besides how soft her skin was.

"You better slow down if you don't want this finished before it gets good, Cadence," he warned.

And that made her laugh. It was a sexy, throaty sound that came from the excitement of her being in total control and knowing it. She loved taking the lead in the bedroom.

"From what I remember, your stamina was never in question, Rory."

"It's been a few months," he defended. "And I missed the hell out of you."

As far as his heart went, Rory didn't normally go there but this was Cadence. She

was his weakness and he was man enough
to admit it.

Yeah, he was pretty much putty in her
hands when it came to sex. And yeah, Cadence was the only person who had that effect
on him. And then there was the simple fact
that their sex had been beyond any experience
he'd had in the bedroom, which was saying
a lot because there'd been plenty of good sex
before her. Since had been the downer. He'd
gone on a few dates, none of which had netted
anything more than boredom and a reminder
of how much he missed her quick wit.

After being with someone he could really
talk to and care about, having sex for sex's
sake had lost its appeal.

And he didn't want to examine the reasons.

Rory didn't want to do anything but bury
himself deep inside Cadence and finally find
his way home again. He wrapped his arms
underneath her legs and stood. She wriggled
her hips, burying him deeper and he released
a guttural groan.

"I missed you, Cadence."

"I missed you, too, Rory."

He walked over to his old bedroom. The
door was open so he dropped to his knees at
the foot of the bed and set her sweet round

bottom on the edge. She tightened her legs around his midsection and dug her nails into his shoulders as she gripped him. Her body was flush with his and her breasts pressed into his chest as she rocked back and forth, as he met her thrust for thrust.

Deeper. Harder. She drove him into a fever pitch.

Rory wrapped lean fingers around her hips, driving faster until both of them were gasping for air, climbing…tension building…muscles cording and straining with a need for release.

He could feel her muscles clench and re-lease around his shaft and that rocketed him toward the edge as she flew over.

His body became a battlefield of electrical impulse.

Bombs detonated inside him, releasing all the pent-up tension.

Cadence's mouth found his and kissed her hard.

"I love you," he said low and under his breath when they finally broke apart in order to catch some air. And that was the problem. He did love her. And sex was tainting his thoughts, confusing him because right then, he wanted to find a way to make a relation-ship work.

It wouldn't.

And his heart was about to be ripped apart a second time.

Chapter Thirteen

"Wake up, sweetheart." Rory's voice was a soft whisper in Cadence's ear as he woke her up from a late-afternoon nap the next day.

She blinked her eyes open slowly.

Rory's face filled her field of vision and her stomach flip-flopped like a champion gymnast. He smiled out of the corner of his mouth but she could see tension written across the lines of his forehead, reminding her of the harsh reality waiting for her.

She didn't want to focus on that now. She'd had a few hours of happiness and she wanted to hold on to that for as long as she could.

"What smells so good?" she asked.

"I made tacos."

"Seriously?" Tacos after the deepest sleep she'd had in months and the best sex of probably her life. She'd have been even more thrilled if she wasn't facing down the reading of her father's will in—she checked the clock on the nightstand—an hour and a half. "You cook?"

"Not a lot. But I can manage a decent meal." He didn't kiss her and she could tell from his expression that he'd constructed a wall. Was he distancing himself because of the threat they faced in a little while?

Rory held up a finger and then returned a few minutes later with a plate and a glass of ice water. He handed over the offerings before making another trip. When he returned he was white-knuckling a coffee mug as he took a sip and sat down on the edge of the bed.

"This looks amazing." She wasted no time taking a bite. It was cooked to perfection. Why didn't she know this about him before? Because neither had ever stuck around long enough after sex to find out, a little voice said. She didn't want to go down that road again. "It's even better than it smells."

Normally, he would at least smile at the admission but he studied the wall next to her like it was a treasure map.

"Everything okay?" she asked, figuring he wouldn't tell her but she wanted to ask anyway. Rory had always held his cards to his chest, even with her.

"I need to protect you and I keep making mistakes that put you at risk," he admitted.

Was he talking to her about something real instead of brushing her off?

"Is it too obvious to point out that I wouldn't be alive if it weren't for you?" She touched his arm and half expected him to pull away. When he didn't, she took it as a positive sign that he wasn't completely shutting down on her. He'd done that, she'd noticed, right before he told her that he couldn't be in a relationship with anyone. The fact that he'd quickly added, *If I could, it would be with you*, had done little to stem the pain.

He shot her a look of appreciation. There was something else behind his eyes, an emotion that looked a lot like shame, and she knew him well enough to realize that he believed he was letting her down.

"You're the best at what you do and I realize this whole situation is in reverse for you. Normally, you're on the offensive and this is pure defense. But I'm alive because of *you* and the babies are safe because of their *dad*." She brought her hand over her stomach protectively. "If there's a problem in all this, it's me. I'm not doing a good enough job remembering. I've been thinking that I might be the key. I mean, if someone's after me then I have to have done something to them, right?"

He'd angled himself toward her and was listening intently. The old Rory would've held tight to his anger and put up a wall too high to climb. She could work with this and they could come up with a solution together.

As he seemed to be taking a minute to soak in what she'd said, she cleaned her plate. After downing a glass of water, she felt more like herself than she had since losing her father.

Was being around Rory calming her overactive mind?

She'd bet on it. As a matter of fact, she'd go all-in. Forgetting him before had been torture and the thought of co-parenting, being close without being together, set her nerves on edge. She'd fallen for Rory the minute she'd seen those wild eyes and untamed hair. She'd also known anything short of setting him free to roam the range would be like placing a choke collar around his neck and chaining him to a tree in the front yard.

But it was his sadness, his loneliness that had touched her somewhere down deep. It had left an imprint on her heart that wasn't so easily shaken off. As much as she didn't want that to be the case, she couldn't deny what she felt.

There was no man who had made her feel smart, sexy and beautiful in the same way Rory had. Even being around him now with no makeup and hips that seemed to grow wider by the day made the world feel right in so many ways. He made her feel desirable.

The heat in the kisses they'd shared blew her mind and had been missing in every other kiss her whole life before him.

Even she knew that they couldn't repeat what had happened last night. *Technically, this morning.* That was obvious. And it was most likely the danger she faced, the reality that Dex or whoever was tracking her might catch up to her that had her craving another night with Rory. That made her want to reach out and touch him, get lost in his arms again.

She excused herself to go to the bathroom to freshen up so she could regain perspective. Because right now, she wanted to pull him down on top of her for another round of mind-blowing sex.

After washing her face and brushing her teeth in a real sink for a change, she returned to the bedroom.

Rory was bent forward, elbows on his knees. He looked up at Cadence; those wild eyes seemed so lost to her. His hair was disheveled and there was stubble on his face. He was in beast mode, detached, and she could see determination on his face.

"What's the plan?" She knew there was one.

She stopped in front of him and he took her hands in his.

"Run away with me. Let's get as far away from Cattle Barge as we can," he said, and there was so much pleading in his steel eyes.

"I want to more than I can say. But if I don't show up tonight, good people, honest people would lose their ability to earn a living. These guys have families and they can't afford to stop working. This is what they know and Hereford is their home."

RORY ADMIRED CADENCE'S sense of sacrifice. Even on her worst day, she was better than most people could ever hope to be.

"I hear what you're saying," he admitted. "Nothing in me wants to march you into that house where I'm afraid there's going to be a trap set. One I might not be able to save you from. You understand what I'm saying?"

She nodded. Standing there, beautiful and determined with the fire in her eyes that said she had to do the right thing, caused the vise-like band around his heart to tighten.

"How would I ever sleep at night if Dale's niece had to be pulled out of the preschool she's in because he couldn't afford to send money to his sister? You know Sara's just starting to match the development of her classmates. That costs money and these men deserve to be paid. They sacrifice so much of their lives living at Hereford instead of living in their hometowns with their families and yet they've always looked after me. Dad has helped a lot of young men, like Rupert Grinnell, our newest hire. If he's off the ranch for too long or out of work, who else will hire him? He's still young but he deserves a chance." She made a lot of sense.

"I can see you've put a lot of thought into it," he admitted.

"Believe me when I say that I'm torn between doing right by you and right by them. The minute I start putting my needs above everyone else's is the day I stop caring about anyone but myself. I definitely don't want these girls to grow up thinking their problems are the only ones that count in life," she said.

Rory snapped his face toward her. "Our girls deserve everything we can give them, and that includes perspective."

It was going to take a minute for him to digest the fact that he was having twin daughters. For now, he had to keep the information on the back burner.

"You think Dex or whoever is after me is going to make his move tonight, don't you?" she asked.

There was no use lying or trying to hide what he knew at a gut level. She deserved to know what she was about to face. "Yes. I think he's going to come in with everything he's got to stop you from walking inside that house. There could be so many things that we can't account for. Extra foot patrols will help but that might not stop them from setting booby traps on the ranch. A lot can go wrong because he's in control, not us. We can do our best to control access to the environment but once a target's location has been identified, the rest becomes easy."

"And we already know he can shoot from a distance," she agreed.

"That rifle would have never been set up like that if he couldn't."

"Do you think Dex is our man? What about those guys who tracked us to your place? How many more can there be?" She was firing a lot of questions at him that he couldn't answer.

"It's an unknown variable, which is an

enemy in a situation like this." Rory's cell buzzed. He fished it out of his pocket and checked the screen. "It's Sawmill."

"I have news," Sawmill started right in.

"Okay. I'm putting you on speaker. I have Cadence Butler with me," he informed the sheriff.

"Good. You'll want to hear this, too, Ms. Butler." He issued a sharp breath before continuing. "We got a hit on the descriptions you gave us of the pair of men in the woods after my deputies canvassed the area. Does the name Martin Jenkins or Randol Fleming sound familiar?"

Cadence looked to be searching her memory. She compressed her lips and her gaze darted around. "No. Not at all."

"They're kin to a new hire on the ranch. Young man by the name of Rupert Grinnell," he informed.

All the color drained from Cadence's face as she whispered, *"Rupert."*

It was impossible to believe that a ranch hand would be involved and especially with how close everyone was.

"He was Dad's last new hire. But how could he possibly be involved?" she asked. "And what problem could he possibly have with me?

I didn't know the guy from Adam before he came on board at the ranch. And all the men were interviewed after Dad's death."

"Mr. Grinnell has an association with a man by the name of David Dexter Henley, who sometimes goes by the name of Dex," the sheriff informed.

So, Dex didn't use a fake name like Rory thought he would have. The man must've panicked and given his nickname.

"Rupert, Martin and Randol are related," Rory pieced together. "Dex is…what?"

"All we know so far is the four men are linked. Means, motive and opportunity are still open for question," Sawmill stated.

"Although, with Grinnell working on the ranch, it's possible that he let the others in," Rory said.

"And that could end his involvement right there. We suspect he might not've given them access knowingly based on reviewing the file of interviews. We're considering all possibilities at this point in the investigation," Sawmill informed.

"Do you have any theories?" Cadence asked.

"I was hoping to gain more information from you in order to fit the pieces together,

Ms. Butler." Sheriff Sawmill's radio beeped and buzzed in the background. "We're in the process of tracking down last known addresses and making a list of family members to investigate. I know this doesn't sound like much and I'd like to be able to give you answers, but this is a big break. It's only a matter of time before we piece the story together and make an arrest."

"Where's Rupert?" she asked.

"We were hoping you could tell us that," he said.

"The information about his family members and address when not on the ranch should be in our files. Ed Staples can provide everything." Cadence was cracking her knuckles and her gaze was darting around wildly, her nervous tics.

"Sometimes witnesses remember something later. If that's the case with you, please call my number directly," Sawmill informed.

This phone call was about to be over.

"I wish we had some idea of why Rupert would be involved in this," Cadence said. "He never struck me as a criminal and our office is good at vetting out unstable people. I know his background is shady but he seemed like an honest kid."

"Hereford has a great reputation for treating employees well and it's widely known that it's not an easy job to get," Sawmill agreed.

Cadence's father had a weak spot for young men who needed a hand up. In Rory's case, he would never have betrayed Mr. Butler. Okay, the irony of that thought smacked him square in the nose. He'd walked out on his relationship with his former employer's daughter and had gotten her pregnant. That wasn't much of a thank-you to the man who'd saved Rory's life.

Rory thanked the sheriff and ended the call.

One look at Cadence and he could see that her mind was reeling from the news.

"How old is Grinnell?" Rory asked.

"He's young," she admitted. "He was barely eighteen when we gave him the job and that was about nine months ago."

"Seems odd a young guy could take the heat of being investigated," Rory said, thinking out loud. "It has me wondering if he knew at the time that he'd allowed someone on the ranch."

"It's possible that he could've been used and not known it. He's a sweet kid who I felt didn't belong in the system," she informed.

"The sheriff will send a deputy to turn

this place upside down at any moment," Rory stated.

"I don't like the fact that there'll be so much chaos on the ranch during the will reading," she admitted.

"Me, either." He put his arm around her and she leaned into him for support. It felt a little too right and she felt his muscles tense. Was he thinking the same thing as she was? Getting too close was going to hurt like hell when this was over. If a criminal had his way, that would be tonight.

That old wall erected between them and she could feel the detachment growing. Was he distancing himself so it would be easier to walk away tomorrow? *Like he'd done before?*

Cadence was an idiot to let her emotions get away from her twice. Especially when Rory had already proven he could disappear at a moment's notice and not look back. The only reason he was in Cattle Barge and at Hereford was because her brothers had summoned him. And she was certain he was itching to get back to the land he loved.

She wasn't being fair to him and on some level, she knew it. Rory hadn't exactly said he wanted to leave.

"Sawmill has a direction and a few names.

Now, it's a matter of tracking those boys down and fitting the pieces together," he stated.

"The sheriff initially said that the top reasons people murder are for greed, anger and revenge," Cadence stated as she stepped away from him. A look of hurt darkened his eyes, but what had he expected? He wasn't the only one who could play the made-of-ice game. Plus, she needed to keep her emotions in check and maintain focus. "If I isolate greed, what could any of these boys hope to gain from Dad's death?"

"Anger seems like it would be more heat-of-the-moment. You come home to find your spouse in bed with the neighbor and lose your cool. You grab the gun in the cabinet before reason can set in and *boom* everyone's life is changed forever," he speculated.

"Revenge is killing someone in cold blood while they slept on their ranch," she said. "Rupert would've had access to my father. But everyone, and I mean *everyone*, was interviewed by the sheriff or one of his deputies. How could he have come out clean? He's young and that's a lot of pressure for someone his age to pull off. He never struck me as a coldhearted criminal and he'd have to be in order to murder the man who was giving him a chance at a better life."

"That's all true and everything depends on his background. There are world-class thieves and liars younger than eighteen," he stated. "Rupert could be in trouble. Someone could've paid him to look the other way."

"Seriously?" She'd read news that supported his accusation but it was almost impossible for her to believe someone like that could slip through Hereford's hiring system.

"I know it's difficult for someone like you to believe," he said.

"What does that mean, *someone like me*?" she scoffed.

"Someone who grew up in the main house," he informed.

"Don't you mean someone who was born with a silver spoon in her mouth?" she snapped.

It was the stress of the situation causing her temper to flair.

"I didn't say that," he defended.

"Why not? Am I too fragile to know the truth of how you really think about me?"

Chapter Fourteen

Cadence could feel her temper rising. It wasn't good for the babies. It wasn't good for her. And it wasn't good for her relationship with Rory. Why did she let his words cut right through her?

"I'm not sure what's going on but I don't want to fight with you, Cadence." Instead of giving as good as he got, Rory's voice was a study in calm. There was compassion there, too.

"Same here."

"The sheriff has names. He finally has suspects. The investigation is about to break apart and your father's murderer will be brought to justice." He glanced toward her belly. "We might have a long road ahead of us and a lot to work out personally between the two of us, but I don't want them to feel stress when they hear you talking to me anymore. I have no idea what they can sense or remember, but we need to be on the same page when it comes to them."

Everything he said made sense. Her emotions were about as overclocked as they could get, which wasn't all Rory's fault. It wasn't right to take out her frustration on him. "I owe you an apology for—"

"None needed," he cut her off.

"Let me finish," she insisted.

He nodded.

"You made a good point. I have no idea what the real reason was for my parents' divorce. Did they fight? Was he unfaithful because of it? I don't even know what my mother was like. We never spoke about her. It was like some unwritten rule that she could never be brought up in conversation. And why? What happened that was so bad?" She paused to stem the flow of emotions and gather the rest of her thoughts. "You and I have a chance to do better. We can get this right for our girls." She paused to take another breath. "I know what we did last night was a mistake and can't happen again. I think we both know how much sex complicates the situation between us."

He nodded but an emotion flickered behind

his eyes. Regret? Sadness? Feelings aside, they both knew what she said was for the best. He'd instinctively pulled away from her, even if he hadn't fully acknowledged it yet.

"I'll always care about you, Rory. We've known each other since we were kids. Nothing's going to change that." Beyond that, her feelings were a hot mess, and she figured pregnancy and hormones were amplifying them.

"Everything you said makes sense," he said after a thoughtful pause. "Kissing you when we're this close is as natural as breathing to me. But that muddies the water and we won't just be hurting ourselves anymore if we go back and forth between friends and…" He looked to be searching for the right word before adding, *"More."*

"We owe it to these girls to find common ground," she stated, hoping her heart would catch up. Everything they were saying was logical.

He glanced at her belly. "I think we did the day we made those two."

There was a huge positive emerging out of all this. Rory seemed to be coming to terms with the fact that he was going to be a parent. It had taken Cadence months to do the same.

"Right now, our main focus needs to be getting you through the next few days until the sheriff can get those boys off the street and get to the bottom of what's happened." There was so much sincerity in his voice.

"Agreed." Her heart fought against the idea of settling into a friendship with Rory. But their feelings were volatile and being a good parent had to come before everything else in her life. "It's about time to go to the main house."

"As soon as I cover our tracks here," Rory said, turning toward the kitchen.

"What if there's evidence here?" she asked.

He stopped midstride. "I'll text Sawmill to let him know where we've been hiding. He'll be able to figure out how to best move forward with his investigation and, hopefully, keep our names out of the report until Grinnell is found."

"It's so tempting to look through his things to see if we can figure out why he would be involved in something like this," she admitted.

"You were right before, though. We can't risk damaging evidence. Not only is it illegal but it can hurt the investigation. I don't want to do anything to make this harder."

Cadence glanced at the clock on the microwave in the open-concept room. "It's getting late."

The severe look that crossed his features before he forced a smile worried her. It meant that the normally confident man was hiding something. Fear? She'd never seen him afraid of anything in his life. In his job, he'd stared down death countless times. But then there'd never been so much at stake before, she thought as she touched her belly.

Rory fished his cell out of his pocket. He punched in a number she recognized as Dalton's.

Her brother picked up on the first ring. He and Rory exchanged greetings and confirmation that she and Rory were safe and doing well.

"There haven't been any attempts on any of us at the ranch," Dalton confirmed. His tone was guarded with Rory now and Cadence regretted insisting on keeping their fling a secret. Her brothers and Rory had been close once and she could see that this had hurt their relationship. Since she was having Rory's daughters, he would be in their lives as family no matter what. She made a mental note that she would have to smooth things over with her family once this was all said and done. She prayed she'd be around to be the one to do it.

"You hear about Rupert Grinnell?" Rory asked.

Dalton issued a grunt along with a strong word under his breath. "Yes."

"Any idea where he is?" Cadence interjected.

"No. He's probably damn lucky I don't," Dalton responded.

Rory glanced at Cadence before asking Dalton, "Where are you right now?"

"I'm heading home. Why?"

"Are you coming from the east or west?" Rory didn't answer Dalton's question yet and Cadence immediately picked up on the reason.

"West." Dalton's voice was tentative.

"Mind a couple of extra passengers?" he asked.

It sounded like it took a second for everything to click in Dalton's mind. "I see what you're saying. Where's a good place to pick up my extra cargo?"

"What's the situation with the reporters?" he asked.

"They're lining the street half a mile on either side of the gate. Seems like they want to be certain they get a shot of anyone coming or going tonight so they're sticking closer to the main entrance," he admitted, and Cadence didn't like the sound of the word *shot*.

"We can make it to the road two miles out and coming in from the west side in twenty minutes," Rory promised. "That work for you?"

"I'll see you both then," Dalton said. Before ending the call, he added, "Cadence…"

"Yes, Dalton."

"I know we gave you a hard time growing up but Dade and I are proud of you. Everyone wants you to know how much we love you."

"I love y'all, too." Tears welled in her eyes. An onslaught of emotion nearly drowned her. Cadence steeled her determination. Crying wouldn't do any good. Focus would. "And I'll see you in twenty minutes."

The call ended with a bad feeling. She didn't like the tone in her brother's voice. It was filled with regret and had a quality that made her think he was afraid he'd never see her again.

THE NIGHT WAS pitch-black and cloudy. A cold front was blowing through and the temperature was expected to drop twenty-five degrees in the next hour. Cadence would be inside the main house long before then, warming up by a nice fire.

Being outside on such a chilly night reminded her of all the times she and her brothers or Ella would sit out back and roast marshmallows over the fire pit.

There was a large tire swing off to one corner of the yard. She'd spent a good portion of her childhood on it during lazy summer days.

When she really thought about her life growing up on a ranch, she remembered how wonderful and different it had truly been. There were so many good times with her siblings. There were fights, too. She never doubted any one of them would have her back if she needed a hand.

If she got bored with her siblings, there were always animals around. The best part about being at Hereford, though, was being surrounded by so many people she loved. What would her life have been like if she hadn't? Would she have felt lonely? Granted, her girls would always have each other.

The thought of bringing up twins on her own while Rory disappeared for weeks, sometimes months, on end hit her like stray voltage. Would she feel lonely? Alone? The freedom that was supposed to come with moving to

Colorado was sounding more like a recipe for isolation. Babies were a lot of work. Could Cadence take care of them on her own?

She would do what she had to, a little voice said.

Would their lives be better at Hereford? May would be here. She would be the closest they'd have to a grandmother since Rory didn't speak to his family. Now she understood his reasoning and she wouldn't try to push him into doing anything he'd be uncomfortable with. Besides, it wasn't her business anyway.

She couldn't help but think it would be nice if the girls had grandparents in their lives, though. Having none was far better than someone who was abusive, don't get her wrong. Since Rory clearly had been close with his sister when they were young, Cadence could urge him to locate Renee. Family was family and she'd take all she could get.

Especially now that she was having a change of heart about living at Hereford. There was plenty of land on which she could build a house for her and her girls. She wanted her babies to have more than her and Rory. Growing up in a loving environment like Hereford would give them a safety net. The past few days had taught Cadence that she couldn't guarantee she would be around.

She didn't want to think about that while she traipsed through the chilly woods again. Rory cut a path for them. He knew exactly what he was doing and where he was going at all times on Hereford.

It might be cold outside but she and Rory had borrowed warm coats from the bunkhouse and only her hands were cold. She blew on them while rubbing them together to stave off the chill.

Rory's phone dinged, which was the signal that Dalton was nearing the pickup spot.

"Let's pick up the pace," he urged.

She followed in his footsteps to keep branches from smacking her in the face as they cut through the woods.

The hum of an engine, the bright lights caused her to gasp.

Nearing the road, seeing the headlights of her brother's vehicle coming toward them, brought on another wave of nostalgia.

Rory linked their fingers before jogging toward it.

The thought of going home to the main house caused a surprising onslaught of emotion to crash down on her.

And then it dawned on her. It was Christmas Eve and her father wouldn't be coming home.

Soon, everyone would know his final wishes.

She put a hand on her belly as the passenger door opened and she slid inside the back of Dalton's vehicle.

"It's good to see the two of you." Stress deepened her brother's voice. "Stay low and I'll get us through security. I pulled a blanket out of the back so you can pull it over your heads. You'll blend in back there and no one will be the wiser."

"Thank you, Dalton. For always looking out for me." She might not have always appreciated her brothers nosing in her business and overprotecting her. Looking back, she realized that their hearts were always in the right place, even if some of their actions were misguided.

Judging her brothers harshly for always having her back seemed overly sensitive now. The pregnancy had changed her perspective on life and family.

She made herself as small as she could on the floorboard, working around the protruding bump without putting undue pressure on her midsection.

"Comfortable?" Rory whispered, readjusting himself in order to give her more room. He took up a lot of space. He was a big guy.

"It's not far. I can make it until we get home," she responded.

Now, all she could do was hope they made it inside the gate safely. Of course, based on what Rory had said about the possibility of the place having traps set, that was only the first step. She had no idea what was waiting for them.

BEING AROUND CADENCE for the past few days reminded Rory of all the reasons he'd fallen for her in the first place, not the least of which was her spunk.

As long as he kept his emotions under control, he figured the two of them would get along fine. But he and Cadence were gasoline and fire when they were together. That same spark made for great conversation and even better sex, both of which had to be tempered now that they were going to be parents of twin girls.

As much as Rory knew better than to let the babies affect his judgment he was already getting attached. The thought of losing Cadence or his girls to some creep sent his blood pressure through the roof.

Since learning he was going to be a father, he'd started thinking about the possibilities of getting more out of life. Could he have a wife and a happy marriage? Was a real family even an option for someone like him? Someone with his background?

Hearing Mr. Butler's words inside his head every time he thought about a future with Cadence wasn't helping. Rory wasn't good enough for her and it would only be a matter of time before she figured it out and left him.

And once again, he reminded himself that his parents were the worst possible fit for each other because of their differences.

Having grown up in what felt like a war zone, he'd vowed long ago never to allow that to happen if he ever had a kid. He was more resolved than ever to keep his feelings for Cadence in check and his eye on the prize— happy children.

That would make her happy, too, in the long run. But then he also realized the irony of his trying to rationalize his feelings toward her. Was it too late?

In walking away from her before he'd not only hurt her but he'd put himself through hell. He'd wanted to forget her, to put her out of his mind, but that had been impossible.

Seeing the way she glowed when she talked about the babies wasn't helping him keep perspective.

People co-parented all the time without letting their feelings for each other run out of control, he reminded himself. He and Cadence could do the same.

Couldn't they?

Chapter Fifteen

Slipping onto the ranch and avoiding journalists seemed like a simple enough plan. Cadence was surprised at how easy it turned out to be. She was reminded of one of May's most frequent sayings that most of the time the simple plan was the right one.

Being home brought so many memories crashing down around her. Cadence exhaled slowly as she heard the garage door closing. Facing Hereford without her larger-than-life father was hard. A band tightened around her chest. For a split second, she wanted to escape. Until she saw his old pickup truck in the bay next to them.

She smiled as she remembered spending a good chunk of her childhood sitting next to him while he drove on the property. He'd tell her to scoot next to him and instruct her to take the wheel just before putting his hands high in the air.

Air from the open windows had blasted her, whipping her hair around as she squealed and gripped the steering wheel.

"It feels good to be home," she said, pulling the rest of the blanket off.

"This is where you should be," Dalton said. It felt so right to hear those words.

"How much time do we have before the reading?" she asked her brother.

He checked his watch. "Ten minutes."

Rory smiled at her. Without much fanfare, he pressed a kiss to her lips. It was tender and sweet and was more intimate than making love in a strange way.

"You're going to be okay. Dalton and your family will make sure of it," he said and then slipped out of the vehicle.

"Wait a minute. You're not coming inside with me?" she asked and then it dawned on her that he was going to check the perimeter and do what he did best...track people.

"I know exactly who I'm looking for and I won't be far," he promised before turning to Dalton, who was standing off to the side. "I owe you and Dade an apology for seeing your sister behind both of your backs. I hope you know that I'll do right by her and our children."

"Children?" Dalton asked with shock in his voice.

"She's pregnant with twin girls," Rory informed him. "I have every intention of being the father they need."

"I never questioned it," Dalton said, and she saw Rory exhale out of the corner of her eye. "Just so you're aware. We were given clear instructions from Ed Staples. Our father requested your presence at the reading."

Rory's jaw fell slack and his eyebrows knitted. "What reason could there possibly be for *me* to be there?"

"Those were the instructions. I have no idea the rhyme or reason. You know my father," Dalton said with a shrug.

"Did he call for other ranch hands?" Rory asked.

"Not to my knowledge and we would've received word before we sent everyone home," Dalton stated.

Leave it to her father to throw a fast-pitch when everyone was expecting a curveball.

"I'd rather be outside, watching the perimeter," Rory admitted.

"There's some kind of stipulation that if you

don't show, the envelope is not to be opened. Ed said he'll have to destroy it," Dalton said. "Aren't you at least a little curious about what our father wanted to say to you?"

Rory stood there for a long moment. There was so much emotion playing out in his features that she could only imagine what was going on inside his head. Her father had been a mentor to Rory. By Rory's account, her father had saved his life. By contrast, Cadence was in danger and that would weigh heavily on Rory's mind. Although he would never speak it aloud, he would never forgive himself if anything happened to her. He was already giving himself a hard enough time for the pregnancy and feeling like he'd backed Cadence against a wall by not being there for her.

"Can the reading start without me?" he asked.

"I believe so. It shouldn't hurt anything if you're late," Dalton said.

"I promise I'll be there," he said to Cadence before slipping out the door.

Rory was a pro. He tracked dangerous men for a living. This was no different.

So why had her nerves tensed?

"Are you ready for this?" Dalton asked with a glance toward her stomach.

"I'm not going to lie. It's hard to be at Hereford without Dad," she admitted, and there was so much relief in finally saying that out loud to one of her family members.

"Holidays are making it tougher," he agreed with a nod.

"It won't be the same without him," she said. "It doesn't even feel like Christmas. Between the pregnancy and…everything that's happened, I haven't done anything to feel in the holiday spirit. I doubt there's anything I could do this year to make it feel normal."

"Same here." Dalton paused in front of the door leading into the main house. "I'm thankful the rest of us are together, though."

He made a good point.

"It might not be the same without him but we have a lot of new family members to look forward to spending the holiday with." Dalton glanced at her stomach with a smile.

"Look at how much has changed in less than a year," she said. "We have a brother and sister we never knew about. And don't even get me started about all the love that's come into everyone's life." She tried not to think about the fact that she was the only single Butler now. Besides, she was thrilled her siblings had found true love and life partners.

It didn't bother her not to be married. Being around all that love made her realize what she was missing in her life, what she would never have with Rory... Stability. He would always have a need to take off and live off the land. Whereas, she wanted a nice house on the ranch and plenty of space to bring up her daughters while being surrounded by the same love she'd known as a kid.

"This past year has taught me how important family is. I guess I've always taken it for granted that we'd be here for each other. Are you still thinking about staying on in Colorado?" he asked.

"How'd you know that?" The only person she'd admitted that to was Rory.

"After all the time you were spending there, it seemed like the next logical step for you," he admitted.

"Not anymore. I'd like to build a small house for me and the girls right here at Hereford, where we belong."

"Sounds like the best idea I've heard all day," he said with a genuine smile before opening the door to their family home.

Ella rushed to the kitchen and wrapped Cadence in a warm hug. May followed, as did the newest Butler sister, Madelyn. Cadence embraced her soon-to-be sisters-in-law, Carrie, Meg and Leanne. Her new brother, Wyatt, wrapped an arm around her and gave her a quick peck on the forehead followed by a protective look. "No one's getting through here while I'm around."

Wyatt fit right in with Dade and Dalton, she thought.

Ed Staples, the family's attorney, padded into the kitchen next. After a hug and a greeting, he glanced up at the clock on the wall. "It's midnight. Time to get started if everyone's ready."

That meant it was Christmas. For a long moment, no one spoke.

Cadence got lost in memories of waiting up with her brothers and sister every Christmas Eve. When the clock struck midnight, they would gather in the main living room, scattering around the Christmas tree. May was there right alongside them with a tray of freshly baked cookies and glasses of milk. Their father would hand out presents and she could see the gleam in his eyes so clearly even now. It was the one time he went overboard and treated them to a stack of presents. He was like a kid himself for that brief time when he helped put together train sets or Hot Wheels tracks and then beamed as he sipped coffee and watched each of his kids with smiles plastered on their faces. They'd stay awake until the sun came up and then crash until supper.

She might not have her father anymore but she had those memories. In an odd way, remembering him made it feel like he was still present and it comforted her.

An instant later, it was like everyone in the room had the same idea at exactly the same time. Synchronicity.

"Merry Christmas," Cadence said to her brother Dade, who had moved next to her before embracing her in a warm hug.

"Merry Christmas, little sis," Dade said before they both moved on to pass holiday greetings onto someone else. Ella and Madelyn hugged and a few tears were shed.

Eventually, everyone filed into the main living area and took seats. Cadence glanced around, wishing Rory was there, too. There was no telling what dangers he faced outside and a thought struck her that something could've happened to him.

He might've encountered Dex or one of the others.

A tree branch scraped across the window, causing her to gasp. Others froze.

It was easy to see that everyone was on edge.

"Thank you to everyone for being here," Ed said. "I know your father would hate to miss a gathering like this and especially on Christmas."

"He always did like a good party," Ella agreed, and those who knew him best chuckled at the fond memory. It was true.

"And he loved to be the center of attention. Although, he'd never admit it," Cadence added.

Heads nodded and smiles brightened everyone's faces. She glanced at Wyatt and Madelyn before realizing they had no memories of their father. How sad was that? To grow up never knowing who their father was. She could help them in that department if they'd let her.

Ed held up a yellow legal-sized envelope and opened the clasp. On a sigh, he said, "Let's begin."

The ticking clock made Cadence's pulse kick up. Where was Rory?

She focused on Ed, trying to block out the fear that something had happened to him.

"To my family,

"First of all, I'd like to wish y'all a Merry Christmas. I'm sorry that I won't be there this year to join you for presents and our traditional meal."

Shocked gasps echoed throughout the large space.

"How on earth is this possible?" Cadence asked under her breath, but others said similar things. "Could he have known all along that he was being targeted for murder?"

Ed gave a noncommittal shrug. "He never said anything to me about it."

When she really thought about it, it was the only thing that made sense. He'd left letters for most of the others that had given them the closure they needed to be at peace with their complicated relationships with him.

But one part didn't add up. Her father had never been the roll-over-and-die type. Why would he let a murderer prance onto the property and shoot him in cold blood?

Logic said he might not've known how or when exactly it was going to happen. But had he expected it? Had he seen it coming somehow?

Once the room quieted down again, Ed continued reading.

"I've never been a sentimental man, but I have loved every one of you in my own way. My biggest regret in life is that I wasn't a good enough father. It's my final hope that you can find forgiveness in your hearts for a foolish man who learned what was truly important a little too late in life."

Ed paused, clearly becoming emotional. He mumbled an apology before continuing.

"To each of my six children I leave equal division of the ranch and my assets with the exception of a million dollars in cash and the main house, both of which go to May Apreas. Her faithful years of service, kindness and generosity have gone well above and beyond the call of duty. I thank you from the bottom of my heart, May."

Smiles wrapped everyone's faces who'd been touched by May. The gifts to her were so well deserved.

Ed explained that rights to the main house would revert to the children following May's death.

"To Dade. I was the hardest on you and could never figure out how to fix it. You are so much like me that it scared me. I didn't want you to make the same mistakes I did. My failed attempts to build a bridge of communication recently are not your fault. They belong to me. I failed you, not the other way around. I am sorry. Forgiveness for my sake is too much to ask. So, do it for yours. It's taken a lifetime for me to figure out that forgiveness is a gift we give ourselves, not the other way around. I hope you can be free of the same burdens I carried that kept me from being able to let everyone know how dear y'all are to me. How proud I am of each one of you."

Sniffles filled the room and there wasn't a dry eye. Not even with the new additions to the family, some of whom had never met him.

Dalton threw an arm around Dade in a brotherly hug and it looked like a weight had been lifted from Dade. He and Cadence were the only two who hadn't received personal messages. Cadence was happy for Dade because he carried around the biggest burden from their childhoods. He and their father had never seen eye to eye or found common ground. The look on Dade's face right now said he had found peace with the past.

Cadence was hoping that her father would be able to shed light on why Dex and the others might have murdered him. How Rupert was involved.

And, selfishly, she wanted to know where her mother was and if he'd stayed in contact with the woman who'd given birth to four of his children.

Ed allowed a few minutes to pause and let everyone gather their emotions. His ruddy cheeks were wet with tears and she figured he missed their father, his friend, as much as everyone else did. In some ways, Ed was probably even closer to their dad, being his best friend and confidant.

He glanced around the room, searching each face, seeming to wait for approval to keep going. He swiped at a tear and nodded before refocusing on the page in front of him.

"I didn't talk about your mother much. Losing her when Cadence was still so young weighed on my conscience. I thought it was best to tell you she'd moved away because I didn't know how to explain to little kids that their mother was never coming back. I thought it would give you hope that you'd see her again someday instead of breaking you down like it did me. It was my guilt eating away at me. Not only was I a bad father but a no-excuse husband. When I lost her, I didn't know how to talk to you about death. I thought it would take away hope.

"Life is odd.

"Now that I'm facing mine, so much more makes sense to me."

Their father knew he was dying? That was the big secret he was going to reveal? The reason for the big changes in his life?

Questions swirled. Their mother had died? She hadn't run off?

Did Ruth know? She must not've because she would've said something. Right?

"When I found out that the pain in my side turned out to be more than a pulled muscle or lower back injury, I realized life is short for everyone. Enjoy your time. Don't waste it on hurt or sorrow. Celebrate more. Let others win sometimes.

"I've wronged a lot of people in my life, including the people who mattered most. A few men will most likely come for me and I'm not going to stop them. Believe me, whatever death they have planned will be so much shorter and less painful than the one nature has dealt. I'm not excusing anyone's behavior. No one should get away with murder. But it's my hope that you can forgive the one who gets to me first. Live your life on your terms and make them good ones.

"I couldn't be prouder of any one of you. Hereford is in the best possible hands.

"With all my love,

"Your father."

Cadence glanced up in time to see Rory standing in the doorway. She pushed up to her feet, met him halfway across the room and buried her face in his chest.

His strong arms wrapped around her and she finally felt like she was home.

"I heard everything," he said low enough for only her to hear. "Your father's right. We have a chance to be better people than our parents. It's time to forgive them and ourselves, and move on."

Chapter Sixteen

Out of the corner of his eye, Rory saw Ed Staples making a beeline toward him. Emotions had been running understandably high in the room and Ed showed that intensity in his expression.

Mr. Butler had been clear in person. Was he worried that Rory hadn't gotten the message to leave his daughter alone? Under the circumstances, Rory wondered if Mr. Butler would feel the same way now that Cadence was pregnant. Guess he'd know in a few seconds.

"This is for you, Mr. Scott." The family lawyer handed Rory an envelope. He glanced at Cadence—for reassurance?—before opening the letter as Ed excused himself from the conversation. He must've realized this needed to be a private moment.

Rory was thankful for the consideration as he unfolded the handwritten note.

Rory,

You remind me so much of my younger self. I've been hard on you. I tried my best to push you away. But the fact that you're reading this now shows me how much you care about my daughter. It's been obvious to everyone that she took a shine to you the minute the two of you met. She was too young and needed a chance to date other people so she would know you were the one if she came back to you. I did everything I could to keep the two of you apart and give her time to grow into herself. I even sent her away to college, hoping she'd meet someone else there.

True love stands the test of time and I knew if the two of you ended up in the same room long enough that you'd find a way to be together.

You'll never know how much time you have with a person. Don't waste it.

And should you and Cadence decide to spend your lives together, I hope you'll take your place alongside the others on the ranch. I'm proud of Hereford. Not because of the money it made. It's done well enough. But for the people I've been able to help along the way. In the beginning, I bought a ranch to make a successful business. I'll admit it. Recently, I've realized that it was the home we built there that has mattered the most.

You have my blessing.

Mr. Butler had been good to Rory. The man was the reason Rory had stayed on the straight and narrow. Having her father's blessing lifted a heavy weight off Rory's shoulders. He needed to find a way to convince Cadence to marry him. He loved her with all his heart and he would trade his life if it meant protecting her and the babies.

With Cadence tucked under his arm, Rory felt like he was finally home.

Now, it was time to figure out why Dex and the others were after Cadence and put them behind bars for their involvement in Mr. Butler's murder. Rory wanted to give that gift to the family for taking him in and always making him feel a part of something real. He figured family was as much a choice as it was a birthright.

Dalton's cell phone buzzed and a hush fell over the room. He glanced at the screen. "It's Terrell."

This wasn't going to be good news.

Dalton answered the call and said a few *uh-huh*'s into the phone.

"Hold on," he said and then lifted his mouth away from the receiver. "There's been a breech. Someone's in the house."

A palpable wave of panic rolled through the room as Rory tucked Cadence behind him.

Everyone backed up until they were huddled together in the center of the space and could see every entrance into the room clearly.

Rory pushed himself up to the front so he could watch the hallway leading to the bedrooms and the laundry room doorway on the other side of the kitchen. Of course, they were all sitting ducks and a good sniper could pick them off one by one.

The sound of glass breaking whirled his attention toward the front window.

The crack of a bullet split the air.

"Get down," Rory commanded as he made himself as large a target as he could by puffing up his body.

Shock registered and he ignored the white-hot pain in his shoulder.

"Get everyone out of here and off the property," he said to Dade and Dalton.

The twins immediately bolted into action, moving the group toward the garage. Rory ducked behind a sofa and belly crawled toward the shooter that he was sure was Dex.

Dex would change locations now that he'd given his position away, so Rory needed to stay low and behind as large of an object as he could find.

One of the twins had the presence of mind to tap the light switch on his way out, plunging the living room/kitchen areas into complete darkness. Rory couldn't see his hand in front of his face. It would take a minute for his eyes to adjust.

Right now, he had the advantage, so he tucked and rolled toward the broken window, knowing full well Dex would've changed positions by now.

It was a chess match. The one with the best moves would win.

The stakes for Rory had never been higher. The Butlers had given him a real family with a real home. He was in love with Cadence and wanted to spend the rest of his life with her bringing up those babies. Being on the range in Wyoming without her had been miserable.

His life had been full of darkness and Cadence was the light.

In facing the possibility of losing the people he cared most about, life became crystal clear. Rory would do what it took to make his family safe. Nothing else mattered.

Rory pulled his backup weapon, a Sig Sauer, from his ankle holster. Sharp stabs of pain radiated from his right shoulder. That would be tricky for a couple of reasons. For one, he already knew he was bleeding badly. He ripped off a piece of his T-shirt to tie off the injury. Felt like the bullet had hit bone but that was the pain talking. Another problem was that being shot on the right shoulder could affect his aim. He needed a steady hand in order to hit his target at a safe distance. He might not have either.

Shouting echoed from the garage and it dawned on him what Dex and his boys were doing. Herding. They'd isolated him from the group and then attacked. He released a string of curse words as he popped to his feet and blasted toward the kitchen. He caught the corner of the solid wood coffee table on his shin, which caused him to stumble.

Quickly regaining his balance, he bolted toward the kitchen door. His eyes didn't need to be completely adjusted to the dark. He knew the layout of the house as well as he did his own cabin. He'd grown up at Hereford. It was home. And it was under siege.

Rory dropped to a crouched position, opened the door leading to the garage and then slipped inside.

A shot blasted his ears and there was more yelling. The sound of a car door slamming shut echoed.

Frantic, he searched the immediate area for the shooter. He dropped down onto his stomach to check for shoes, peeking under the carriage of the trucks. Cadence had had on the hiking boots he'd purchased for her. He scanned the area for any sign of the brown boots. Hope died in his chest when he saw there were none.

He couldn't shout at anyone because that would give away not only his position but also anyone's who answered.

Popping to his feet burned his thighs but it was his shoulder that was causing the blinding pain.

Progressing forward, he located a small group that was huddled together.

"Where is she?" he whispered to Dalton who was protecting the small group.

"With Dade maybe?" Dalton responded in a hushed tone.

Rory located Dade next and asked the same question. His heart clenched when Dade told him to ask Dalton.

All commotion had ended and silence belted Rory across the face like a physical punch.

A full search of the garage revealed she wasn't there.

Cruiser lights along with sirens lit up the night sky as Rory ran outside. His gaze darted across the expansive yard, searching for her. There was nothing. He checked the ground for any signs of her.

Did she break away? Run?

It was almost too much to hope that she'd gotten away and was biding her time until Dex and his men were caught.

Or was it? She knew the land as well as anyone.

He picked up on a set of footprints going out to the barn. The imprints in the heels were a match to Cadence's boots. The deep imprint suggested she was running. So this was recent.

The image of her hunkering down against the frigid night air, trying to keep herself from freezing, assaulted Rory. Other images crossed his mind that he couldn't allow to take seed because they had her in a trunk somewhere with a bullet in her forehead.

Rory focused on the first possibility. The one that had her sleeping outside at night with no coat or covers. So much for improvement.

And then he realized the tracks stopped. He scanned the area for a second set or any signs of a struggle.

The doctor had told her to rest and he worried that more stress could cause her to lose the babies, *their babies.* Waves of anger vibrated through him.

A noise to his left sounded. Rory froze. It wasn't much more than wind whistling through barren trees but he heard it.

The unmistakable sound of a heavy shoe on a branch caught his attention next.

Rory crouched low, his movement soundless. Based on the weight of the footsteps, Rory was dealing with a male. He could also tell the person was being quiet intentionally, signaling the man was hunting. The man— Dex?—would take a few steps and then listen. After another few steps, he would stop to listen again.

What if Dex or one of his men were watching Rory?

And that's when Rory realized that tracking Cadence could bring the killer right to her.

Rory had a decision to make. His instincts said go after Dex and stop him. The sheriff hadn't caught him yet and if Rory walked away now, Dex could go free.

Before Rory could debate his next actions, Dex came into his field of vision. It was clear that Rory had the element of surprise on his side because Dex didn't so much as tilt his ear toward him. Dex liked to hide in the woods and shoot, which convinced Rory that he didn't trust going one-on-one with an opponent. Rory had him in height and build.

He waited until he could see Dex's chest move when he breathed before he made his move. And then Rory burst from behind the tree, tackling Dex at the knees. The smaller guy toppled over and Rory landed on top.

A fist connected with Rory's chin. His head snapped back and it took a second to register the pain radiating from his jaw. The loss of blood combined with the constant bite coming from his shoulder weakened him. He needed to make a mental adjustment for that as Dex bucked, trying to tip him off balance.

Rory threw a punch but his right side was too weak to make the impact he wanted. He felt around for a rock, anything he could use to knock Dex out.

Dex got off a few punches to Rory's midsection.

Thinking that this was the man who was trying to take Cadence away from him and harm his children gave Rory the burst of adrenaline he needed to power through the blinding pain and focus on stopping Dex.

He fired off several punches, connecting with Dex's face, chest and upper arms.

Dex's head snapped from side to side, taking the impact of everything Rory had left inside him to give. After a few more jabs, Dex finally dropped his arms and fell slack.

To make sure he'd debilitated his enemy, Rory fired off one more punch. When he was certain that Dex was not a threat, he rolled off and onto his back. His breathing was ragged and all he could see was dots.

He fished out his cell phone and called Sawmill to give his location before he passed out. Sawmill answered on the first ring. Rory immediately relayed his location.

"Rupert Grinnell turned himself in an hour ago. He had no idea his cousins were involved last summer with this character who goes by the name Dex. According to Mr. Grinnell, David Dexter Henley's mother claims to have had a relationship with Mr. Butler. Mr. Butler refused to acknowledge Dex as his child and she had a difficult life bringing up the child on her own. Dex talked to his associates about having a DNA test that confirmed he was an heir to the Butler estate. His associates said that he later said that Mike Butler needed to pay for walking out on Dex and his mother. They're assuming he murdered Mike Butler in order to draw the inheritance his father threatened to tie up in court should Dex try to claim it. Mr. Grinnell stated that Dex walked right past Cadence when she was leaving the barn the night of her father's murder." Sawmill paused.

"Meaning as soon as she realized it, she'd be able to positively ID him and testify," Rory said.

"The man became obsessed with tracking her down and said she needed to die so she couldn't identify him, according to his known associates. Mr. Grinnell said his cousins came to him once they realized how far the situation had gotten out of control and the three of them hatched a plan to disappear. David Dexter Henley had threatened them into doing his bidding in the first place and they were afraid of disobeying his orders."

Rory sighed in relief. The others were in custody. Dex was three feet away from him, still knocked out.

And then he heard a noise.

"Is one of your men near me?" he whispered into the phone.

"No," Sawmill admitted.

"Then I gotta go."

Rory listened intently, trying to discern the noise that could mean the difference between life and death.

The footsteps were definitely softer this time, so he hedged that it might be Cadence. Maybe he was hearing what he wanted—plain and simple hope—because he was about to pass out and his life might depend on being the one to wake first. Law enforcement was on its way. Rory fought against the blackness overwhelming him as he strained to listen.

More soft steps.

And then he heard the gasp that could only belong to Cadence.

His heart felt bigger than his chest, barely contained by his rib cage when her beautiful face came into view.

"Are you hurt?" he asked.

"No. I'm fine. Cold but good," she admitted. A look of panic crossed her features when she scanned his body and he instantly knew he must look in bad shape.

"Rory." She dropped down to his side. Her gaze shifting between Dex and Rory.

"It's done. A deputy is on his way. Rupert's cousins confessed and all three went to the sheriff's office to turn themselves in. All three are in custody. Rupert had no idea what was going on," he informed her. The look of relief on her face was short-lived.

"What about you, Rory?" Her gaze surveyed his shoulder and then his face. "Are you in pain?"

Tears welled in her eyes but her chin jutted out in defiance. She was trying to be strong for him.

He stared into her eyes so she would know just how serious he was about what he planned to say next. "I'll be fine the minute you agree to be my wife."

Her chin faltered.

"Before you answer, hear me out." His face pinched in pain as he tried to move his right arm to take her hand in his. Contact sent a bolt of lightning straight to his heart.

"You're hurting, Rory. Don't move." More tears welled in Cadence's eyes, a few spilling over and staining her cheeks.

"I wanted to ask your brothers first," he began and she shot him a warning look.

"I'm perfectly capable of making my own decisions about who I spend time with," she countered.

He smiled at her spunk, even though it hurt like hell.

"Believe me, I know. But I want to do this the right way. No more going behind people's backs. I already have your father's blessing." He patted his jeans pocket with his left hand.

At least she smiled at that, though it didn't reach her eyes.

"If you'll have me, I'm asking you to marry me. You're all the family I need in this life. You and those babies *are* my life. You're the only person I want to come home to every night. The one I can't wait to see first thing in the morning. I want us to be an official family, Cadence." His normal confidence waned. "What do you say? Will you do me the honor of becoming my wife?"

Tears free-fell now and he couldn't tell if that was a good thing or not. His breath stuck in his throat.

"I've loved you since the day I met you, Rory Scott. But I have to ask, what's changed? You still love the outdoors and you'll always see me as some sort of princess."

"That's where you're wrong. I've always treated you as an equal. I never thought I was good enough for you before. If you tell me that I am, I promise to believe you. All I really need to know is that you love me. I want to do right by you, Cadence. My life for the past five months without you has been pure hell. There's nothing on the range that can compete with the way I feel for you. You and those babies are all I really need for a good life, a happy life," he said.

Cadence's face broke into a smile. "I love you. I know who you are and I'll be your wife on one condition."

"Which is?"

"You have to stay true to yourself. I love you the way you are and I wouldn't dream of keeping you indoors or changing you in any way." Her tears stemmed. "Plus, if you change for my sake, you'll resent me."

"That's where you're wrong, Cadence. I'm changing because I'm in love and I want to be with you. And there's no better place than holding you when going to bed at night, comfy sheets and all."

The sound of hurried footsteps broke into the moment.

"So much has changed in the past year," she said. "The family has suffered a terrible loss but I realized something earlier. We've gained so many new faces and so much love. I don't want to dwell on the past. I want to walk toward our future. Together with our girls."

"I love you, Cadence Butler," Rory said as the squawk of a deputy's radio cut into the night air.

"Save your energy," Cadence said. "Help is almost here and I want you back to full form soon so I can marry you."

"As long as you agree to let us keep Boots," Rory said. His heart filled with love for the woman by his side as she smiled.

"I insist we keep him," she said.

"Merry Christmas, Cadence."

"Merry Christmas." She leaned toward him and pressed her lips to his.

He kissed her as he touched her belly. This was his family. He was home.

Epilogue

Rory turned to his wife. He'd never openly admit the look was meant to steel his nerves. Admitting weakness had never been his strong suit. Seeing Cadence's face and quiet strength offered the reassurance he needed to take the next couple of steps toward the old bungalow-style house that needed a fresh coat of paint.

While April showers brought May flowers in many parts of the country, the first of May promised plenty of thunderstorms in Texas and the skies were welling up with clouds. The air was thick and heavy. His hospital visit and recovery were long behind him.

Cadence looked even more beautiful—if that was possible—holding their eight-week-old daughter Katie in her arms. Rory held the other bundle, Kelly, who was swaddled in a pink blanket. Two miracles. Three counting his wife.

Rory wasn't sure how he'd gotten so lucky, but he didn't plan to waste his good fortune.

"I can't wait to meet them," Cadence said. She'd taught him so much about forgiveness in the past five months.

"I hope it turns out to be a good thing." In forgiving others, the darnedest thing happened. He was finally able to forgive himself. For all of it. For the feeling of letting his mother down by not being able to stop his father from hurting her. For the feeling that he'd let Cadence down.

Rory stepped onto the porch. The boards creaked under his weight. The whole place could use some repairs, he noted. Easy enough to send a contractor over to help out if his parents would agree. He had no idea what mood they'd be in and part of him—a big part—had been holding off on making this house call because he hadn't wanted to expose Cadence and the girls to his parents' unpredictability. Cadence had made the phone call asking to meet his parents. He'd been planning to do it, putting it off, but she'd beat him to the punch. That summed up his wife on so many levels. She wasn't one to shy away from a difficult situation. She'd put up with him and had agreed to spend the rest of her life with him. Again, he thought about how lucky he was.

Before he could knock, the door swung open and his mother stood there with a wide smile on her face. She looked surprisingly good. She wore a sleeveless dress. His gaze immediately swept her arms for bruises. There were none.

"Come inside," she said, opening the door wide.

Rory saw his father standing behind his mother. He, too, wore a big smile. Everything looked copacetic but looks could be deceiving.

"Do you want to come in, son?" his father asked, seeming to catch on to his hesitation.

Rory glanced at the grouping of rockers on the porch. "How about sitting outside?"

He wasn't ready to walk into that house again, a house that had brought so much pain, frustration and sorrow.

His mother nodded, still smiling as she wiped a tear from her cheek.

"You okay?" he asked, stepping aside so she could come out.

"It's just so good to see you again," she said as more tears sprang to her eyes. She quickly apologized as he wrapped an arm around her.

"Same here," his father grumbled. He seemed to be fighting emotions, too.

"This is my wife, Cadence." There was so much pride in his voice that he could hear it.

Cadence beamed at his parents. "So nice to meet you both."

She was warmth and sunshine wrapped up into one as she exchanged greetings with his parents.

"It's wonderful to meet you." His mother beamed right back. "She's beautiful, Rory. Looks like she can keep you on your toes."

His father introduced himself before giving her a hug. It was odd to Rory but he liked what was happening with his folks.

"Who do we have here?" his mother asked, nodding toward the baby in his arms.

"Kelly. And over there is Katie." He nodded toward the other pink bundle.

His father shoved his hands in his pockets and shuffled his feet as he moved next to Cadence.

"Please, take a seat wherever you want," he said before smiling at his own wife. He took his right hand out of his pocket and put his arm around Rory's mother.

"Those are our grandbabies," he said quietly and with a reverence Rory had never heard from his father before. Was it true? Had the man changed? Rory wanted to believe it was possible and signs pointed toward it being true.

He searched his mother's arms for bruises again and saw none. Relief washed over him, because he was no longer a child and wouldn't be able to hold his tongue as a man.

Was it possible his parents had changed?

Rory took a seat after Cadence. His parents took a bench, sitting next to each other as they held hands.

"Do you talk to Renee? I plan on tracking her down next," he said as his mother peered at Katie with a huge smile practically plastered on her face.

"We found her last year. She's making music in Nashville with Rodney," his mother supplied.

"She followed her dream. That's cool." It was cool, and he applauded his sister for making good on her plans.

His mother shrugged. "You should hear them. The band's called… Oh, shoot, Henry, what's the name?"

Rory's father put his hands together in his lap. "What are they calling themselves now? Sudden-something."

"No, I think that was the name of the last one. The lead singer took off. They'd been doing backup vocals and making good money, too. But he wanted to take his act solo, so they decided to do their own thing and jobs lined up for them," she supplied. "Oh, I know. It's called, Double Dose of Dixie."

His father was rocking his head.

"She and Rodney have a son. He's the cutest thing with curls for days." His mother's eyes lit up when she talked about Renee and her family.

"How old is he?" It was strange to think of his sister as a mother. Rory almost laughed. No stranger than him being a father when he really thought about it.

"He's five-years-old. They call him Rory Daniel," his father supplied.

That news punched him in the chest.

"I should've stayed in touch," he admitted.

"She says the same thing," his father said. He fished his cell phone out of his pocket.

"Oh, yeah, show him the pictures," his mother urged.

After a few swipes on the screen, his father handed over the phone. Cadence leaned in and Rory marveled at the five-year-old kid with the gap-toothed smile.

"He looks just like your pictures at that age," his mother said proudly.

"He's beautiful," Cadence agreed. "I hope our girls get those curls."

Being back at home was nicer than Rory had expected it to be.

"She happy?" he asked his mother.

"I believe so," she responded. "I mean, look at them. They live in Nashville and she's making music. They're doing pretty well financially. It's not like they're making the kind of money some of the bigger acts make but it's enough to make a good living, to make a home."

"And how about the two of you?" he pressed. "Are you happy?"

His father leaned back and slowly put his arm around his wife. "Losing our kids taught us a thing or two about how our actions affect everyone around us. I quit drinking not too long after you left."

His mother perked up. "He went to one of those AA meetings and before you knew it, we were in counseling." Her eyes sparked in a way he'd never seen before. She seemed happy. "We would've reached out to you a long time ago but we had no idea how to reach you."

"I've been out of touch. I used to be a tracker. I hunted poachers. Not being able to locate me told me I was doing my job well," he admitted.

"Doesn't matter, son. You're here now. And your mother and I..." He hesitated. "*I owe you an apology. When I should've been a father, a husband, I was too busy trying to hide my own pain. Guess I thought I could drink it away, but that only made it worse." He leaned forward and rested his elbows on his knees. "I'll never be perfect, but I'd like to be part of your life. I understand that might take some time after the wrongs I did. I've changed and... I hope that someday I'm half the man you turned out to be."

"As far as the apology goes, I accept," Rory said. "Forgiveness is something I'm learning from my wife. I'm still a work-in-progress. But getting to know the two of you sounds good to me."

"I should've made iced tea so we can toast," his mother said. "Well, here goes nothing." She held out her hand as though holding on to a glass. "To second chances."

"And new beginnings," Cadence said, pretending to clink the imaginary glasses. "And most of all, to love." She looked at each of his parents and then beamed at their daughters.

Rory could toast to that. To love. To the loves of his life.

And to the future ahead of them, which was something he'd always believed would be out of reach for a man like him—a real family.

* * * * *

Look for more books from USA TODAY *bestselling author Barb Han coming 2019.*

And don't miss the previous titles in the Crisis: Cattle Barge miniseries:

Sudden Setup
Endangered Heiress
Texas Grit
Kidnapped at Christmas
Murder and Mistletoe

Available now from Harlequin Intrigue!

Get 4 FREE REWARDS!

We'll send you 2 FREE Books plus 2 FREE Mystery Gifts.

Harlequin® Romantic Suspense books feature heart-racing sensuality and the promise of a sweeping romance set against the backdrop of suspense.

FREE
Value Over
$20

YES! Please send me 2 FREE Harlequin® Romantic Suspense novels and my 2 FREE gifts (gifts are worth about $10 retail). After receiving them, if I don't wish to receive any more books, I can return the shipping statement marked "cancel." If I don't cancel, I will receive 4 brand-new novels every month and be billed just $4.99 per book in the U.S. or $5.74 per book in Canada. That's a savings of at least 12% off the cover price! It's quite a bargain! Shipping and handling is just 50¢ per book in the U.S. and 75¢ per book in Canada.* I understand that accepting the 2 free books and gifts places me under no obligation to buy anything. I can always return a shipment and cancel at any time. The free books and gifts are mine to keep no matter what I decide.

240/340 HDN GMYZ

Name (please print)

Address   Apt. #

City   State/Province   Zip/Postal Code

Mail to the Reader Service:
IN U.S.A.: P.O. Box 1341, Buffalo, NY 14240-8531
IN CANADA: P.O. Box 603, Fort Erie, Ontario L2A 5X3

Want to try 2 free books from another series! Call 1-800-873-8635 or visit www.ReaderService.com.

---

*Terms and prices subject to change without notice. Prices do not include applicable taxes. Sales tax applicable in N.Y. Canadian residents will be charged applicable taxes. Offer not valid in Quebec. This offer is limited to one order per household. Books received may not be as shown. Not valid for current subscribers to Harlequin® Romantic Suspense books. All orders subject to approval. Credit or debit balances in a customer's account(s) may be offset by any other outstanding balance owed by or to the customer. Please allow 4 to 6 weeks for delivery. Offer available while quantities last.

Your Privacy—The Reader Service is committed to protecting your privacy. Our Privacy Policy is available online at www.ReaderService.com or upon request from the Reader Service. We make a portion of our mailing list available to reputable third parties that offer products we believe may interest you. If you prefer that we not exchange your name with third parties, or if you wish to clarify or modify your communication preferences, please visit us at www.ReaderService.com/consumerschoice or write to us at Reader Service Preference Service, P.O. Box 9062, Buffalo, NY 14240-9062. Include your complete name and address.   HRS19

Get 4 FREE REWARDS!

We'll send you 2 FREE Books
plus 2 FREE Mystery Gifts.

Harlequin Presents® books feature a sensational and sophisticated world of international romance where sinfully tempting heroes ignite passion.

FREE Value Over **$20**

YES! Please send me 2 FREE Harlequin Presents® novels and my 2 FREE gifts (gifts are worth about $10 retail). After receiving them, if I don't wish to receive any more books, I can return the shipping statement marked "cancel." If I don't cancel, I will receive 6 brand-new novels every month and be billed just $4.55 each for the regular-print edition or $5.55 each for the larger-print edition in the U.S., or $5.49 each for the regular-print edition or $5.99 each for the larger-print edition in Canada. That's a savings of at least 11% off the cover price! It's quite a bargain! Shipping and handling is just 50¢ per book in the U.S. and 75¢ per book in Canada.* I understand that accepting the 2 free books and gifts places me under no obligation to buy anything. I can always return a shipment and cancel at any time. The free books and gifts are mine to keep no matter what I decide.

Choose one: ☐ **Harlequin Presents®**
Regular-Print
(106/306 HDN GMYX)

☐ **Harlequin Presents®**
Larger-Print
(176/376 HDN GMYX)

Name (please print)

Address   Apt. #

City   State/Province   Zip/Postal Code

Mail to the **Reader Service:**
IN U.S.A.: P.O. Box 1341, Buffalo, NY 14240-8531
IN CANADA: P.O. Box 603, Fort Erie, Ontario L2A 5X3

Want to try 2 free books from another series! Call 1-800-873-8635 or visit www.ReaderService.com.

---

*Terms and prices subject to change without notice. Prices do not include applicable taxes. Sales tax applicable in N.Y. Canadian residents will be charged applicable taxes. Offer not valid in Quebec. This offer is limited to one order per household. Books received may not be as shown. Not valid for current subscribers to Harlequin Presents books. All orders subject to approval. Credit or debit balances in a customer's account(s) may be offset by any other outstanding balance owed by or to the customer. Please allow 4 to 6 weeks for delivery. Offer available while quantities last.

Your Privacy—The Reader Service is committed to protecting your privacy. Our Privacy Policy is available online at www.ReaderService.com or upon request from the Reader Service. We make a portion of our mailing list available to reputable third parties that offer products we believe may interest you. If you prefer that we not exchange your name with third parties, or if you wish to clarify or modify your communication preferences, please visit us at www.ReaderService.com/consumerchoice or write to us at Reader Service Preference Service, P.O. Box 9062, Buffalo, NY 14240-9062. Include your complete name and address.

HP19

Get 4 FREE REWARDS!

We'll send you 2 FREE Books _plus_ 2 FREE Mystery Gifts.

FREE Value Over **$20**

Both the **Romance** and **Suspense** collections feature compelling novels written by many of today's best-selling authors.

YES! Please send me 2 FREE novels from the Essential Romance or Essential Suspense Collection and my 2 FREE gifts (gifts are worth about $10 retail). After receiving them, if I don't wish to receive any more books, I can return the shipping statement marked "cancel." If I don't cancel, I will receive 4 brand-new novels every month and be billed just $6.74 each in the U.S. or $7.24 each in Canada. That's a savings of at least 16% off the cover price. It's quite a bargain! Shipping and handling is just 50¢ per book in the U.S. and 75¢ per book in Canada.* I understand that accepting the 2 free books and gifts places me under no obligation to buy anything. I can always return a shipment and cancel at any time. The free books and gifts are mine to keep no matter what I decide.

Choose one: ☐ **Essential Romance**
(194/394 MDN GMY7)
☐ **Essential Suspense**
(191/391 MDN GMY7)

Name (please print)

Address   Apt. #

City   State/Province   Zip/Postal Code

Mail to the **Reader Service:**
IN U.S.A.: P.O. Box 1341, Buffalo, NY 14240-8531
IN CANADA: P.O. Box 603, Fort Erie, Ontario L2A 5X3

Want to try 2 free books from another series! Call 1-800-873-8635 or visit www.ReaderService.com.

*Terms and prices subject to change without notice. Prices do not include applicable taxes. Sales tax applicable in NY. Canadian residents will be charged applicable taxes. Offer not valid in Quebec. This offer is limited to one order per household. Books received may not be as shown. Not valid for current subscribers to the Essential Romance or Essential Suspense Collection. All orders subject to approval. Credit or debit balances in a customer's account(s) may be offset by any other outstanding balance owed by or to the customer. Please allow 4 to 6 weeks for delivery. Offer available while quantities last.

Your Privacy—The Reader Service is committed to protecting your privacy. Our Privacy Policy is available online at www.ReaderService.com or upon request from the Reader Service. We make a portion of our mailing list available to reputable third parties that offer products we believe may interest you. If you prefer that we not exchange your name with third parties, or if you wish to clarify or modify your communication preferences, please visit us at www.ReaderService.com/consumerschoice or write to us at Reader Service Preference Service, P.O. Box 9062, Buffalo, NY 14240-9062. Include your complete name and address.

STRS19

READERSERVICE.COM

Manage your account online!

- Review your order history
- Manage your payments
- Update your address

> ### We've designed the Reader Service website just for you.

Enjoy all the features!

- Discover new series available to you, and read excerpts from any series.
- Respond to mailings and special monthly offers.
- Browse the Bonus Bucks catalog and online-only exculsives.
- Share your feedback.

Visit us at:

ReaderService.com

RS16R